HAIR OF A FALLEN ANGEL

Hair Of A Fallen Angel

Susan Isla Tepper

SPUYTEN DUYVIL
New York City

© 2024 Susan Isla Tepper
ISBN 978-1-963908-32-9
Author photo by Laura Bruno
Cover image courtesy of Shutterstock

Library of Congress Control Number: 2024946079

To my brother, Chris

CHAPTER ONE

Brother Sly is serving out his time doing clean-up and general duties at the barbershop. Under the circumstances, what with the virus, and the jails filled to the brim, and Brother Sly being one of those religious types they couldn't quite tap—though the newspapers called it *a crime against nature*—well—Judge Henry and the priest had a pow-wow. The papers said they *struck a deal*. In the end, Mel got Sly at the barbershop—for Sly's parole; or whatever you want to call it. Melville owns the shop. Judge Henry must have something really big on Mel. Anyway, hearing he got stuck with Sly, Mel had screamed like murder saying the Judge and the priest should be locked in the asylum on the Georgia border.

I keep my mouth shut. I'm just here to clip toenails off men too old or out of shape to bend over and do it for themselves. I've met some tough yellow nails. It's a service Mel has offered, since, like, forever. Including a hot scented towel on the face for the happy ending. I clip toes and lay towels and listen to complaints all day about Sly doing this or that incorrectly.

By ten-thirty no sign of Sly. Mel is fuming. He doesn't want him but now he'll have to take on Sly's assigned tasks himself. *Menial labor* he spits out; his face gone hot as red liver. I want to say: You know what, Mel, I can easily do whatever Sly does. I can sweep the hair and push it toward the hair drain, AJAX the sinks, tidy up in general.

I sure could use the extra money. Living in that two roomer down by the swamp, mosquitoes feasting before you know they've landed—I'm pretty damn desperate. A clean compact mobile home would put a big smile on my face.

Mel is having twenty-two fits. "Where's that good for nothin' petit-four?" he screams.

I want to scream back: *Pedophile! Pedophile! Just say what you damn well mean!*

Around here everyone beats around the bush. They know; have known forever. With that stuff it's only a matter of time. I look toward the window where the sun coming in is almost a flare. Mel could hang a blind— but no! It's summer and hot as blazes yet I can feel change blowing in. I should look up my horoscope. He keeps the newspaper on top of the step-to garbage bin.

"I can pick up for Sly," I tell him.

Mel shoots me a suspicious look.

"Just for today," I add quickly. Jesus! Does he think I'm in on some deal with Sly? But right now he's got no choice 'cause Bucky Fuller just stepped in booming his wide hello. Someone has to drape him in the chair.

"Go on, Janelle." Mel's squinting at me. "Just for today."

Bucky heaves himself into the middle chair. This way if two more customers come in, Bucky's guaranteed everyone's full attention.

I take a drape off the wall hook and place it across him, tying the back loops at his neck. He looks up and winks. "Thank you sweet cakes." Not a word to Mel about where is Sly. They're all more relaxed when he's not around.

"Hot day," Mel says.

"The whole enchilada," Bucky says. Meaning shave and a hair cut. Hot towel to finish. Does he want his nails clipped?

"Janelle, get the lime shave cream, would ya."

"Sure Mel."

In the back cabinet where the shave creams and

shampoos are stacked in nice packaging, I take out a lime foam, then grab a few more drapes and a couple of towels. I'm picturing that tidy trailer on the uphill side of town.

Bucky calls me sweet cakes again when I place the shave stuff on the portable side stand. I give him a little smile and move away. I'm hoping he doesn't want his nails cut. He and Melville (Bucky calls him by his full name) get into some boring chat. I turn on the radio always set at the same music station.

The same. Always the same. It can drive some people crazy. Maybe it drove Sly nuts and now he's far away living in some city where no one has a clue. But like the judge said (according to Mel) *They always repeat. It's a sickness.*

Bucky gives me a two dollar tip after he pays his bill.

"I like the way you comport yourself, darlin'. You class up this place. Not like that..."

Mel snort laughs.

I don't feel Bucky's words or his cheap tip require anything more than a *Thank you.* God forbid I should lead him on. Not that he'd be capable of much of anything. I hold back a giggle picturing him hoisting his bow-legged self over some poor woman.

The morning drags. I stand at the trash bin reading the paper. Nothing much exciting. No sleaze stories today about which movie star has cheated or who is getting divorced.

Two more customers come in. I have to clip both. Down on my knees, one guy has nails like curved steel. Why some nails grow straight out and others don't is a mystery. Even with the large size clippers, my hand cramps during the process. It's a process. I saw a TV show about that type of psychological thinking. When things are less than satisfactory, you tell yourself over and over *It's a process*. It helps to convert your brain waves from negative to positive. It helps most of the time, except when the roof lets go during heavy rain. Then I have to run around setting down buckets, thinking I should have given Clyde more of a chance. Then the rain stops, and so do all thoughts of Clyde. He was a lousy husband. It's a process.

When the firehouse sounds the noon whistle I say to Mel, "I'm getting a plate from Kenny Rogers. You want anything?"

The shop is dead right now. People here scarf down lunch like it's their Lenten *give-it-up* come to an end meal.

Mel gives me that squint again. "You gettin' a whole plate? Not just a sandwich?"

What's it to him? I shake back my hair which is my stall tactic. Also, puckering my lips. "Thought I'd treat myself today with some chicken and biscuits. They do a nice gravy."

He's looking kind of funny. Like I said I was getting caviar and champagne. "Mel, is there a problem?"

He throws up his hands. "No! No! No problem whatsoever. Just that you always eat little foods like those salads and half a sandwich." He still has that odd look. "Bucky must've tipped you plenty."

"He gave me two fucking dollars."

"OK! I was just jokin'."

Except he wasn't. Does he think we have a little side thing going? Me and Bucky Fuller? "I just lost my appetite," I say.

"Now, listen Janelle, you go on over to Kenny Rogers and sit yerself down at a nice table and eat your chicken and biscuits in the super-cool air conditionin'." He tries out a grin. "And, you take your sweet ole time." When I don't respond with an all-is-forgiven smile, he groans. "Look. I got to get downstairs and pull out all the hair from the trap before the Chinese wig guy gets here. Now go on, Janelle! Shoo!"

I look down at my own shoe. The one coming apart at the side seam on account of a bunion the size of an almond. I could use a new pair, like those cute Skechers they advertise on HSN. Lots of color choices and patterns. I don't have cash to spare.

If I had long, straight-as-a-stick hair I'd chop it off and sell it to the Chinese wig guy in a heartbeat. Mine is red as carrots, thick, wild with curls. To get on my soft side, after he'd fucked up, Clyde used to bury his face in my hair saying *hair of a fallen angel*—some song lyric or something he picked up somewhere.

Mel hands me the soiled towels. "Throw them in the washer before you go out. Use the cold cycle. Half the soap powder indicated."

Everyone knows you have to use hot water. Especially under these current conditions which nobody here talks about. Like that virus is some Martian living in a craft that will not cross the state line. Except, it already has. A breath-sucking Martian that's making tracks through this very county as we stand here talking about towels. I want to scream at him: Get vaccinated! You don't believe? Ask Mae Lewis who lost her husband and oldest boy to that same Martian back in June.

Of course I do none of that. I gather up my sack purse and leave the shop. I don't go to Kenny Rogers. I walk the baking streets of this town thinking: *Let Mel and the guys fend for themselves. Cut their own damn nails. Drape themselves in those plastic capes decorated with the Confederate flag.*

CHAPTER 2

Eventually, I wander over to the fairgrounds. For this town it's equivalent to The Mall of America. I've seen that mall on TV and it's big on my wish list. And bigger than the whole downtown of this damn place.

The fairgrounds stay open all year including Christmas. I make my way through the flattened stumble grass. Sooner or later, with not much else to entice folks, they find themselves over here to buy a cone or can of pop, some hot dogs and corn chips, to see the Ferris Wheel gleaming against the sky for the umpteenth time. A Ferris Wheel that's known some serious action. Once, a drunk stood up and plunged to his death. I never saw that take place though it's legendary. For a while there was a sign erected to honor the dead man. Then AA got all over their case so the sign was taken down.

Over by KNOCK THE DUCK IN THE POND I spot Chillin' Millie on a high wooden stool. She likes to hang out there talking with Hank who owns the attraction. Hank, recently divorced, is nervous about his meal situation. *Connie was a great cook*, he says repeatedly. Never once does he say *I miss Connie so bad*. He misses his great meals on schedule.

I saunter over. "Hey there, Hank."

The divorce caused a flare-up in his psoriasis; I watch him scratching his arm to the beat of some canned music coming from the attraction one over. His brow is furrowed. Business being slow isn't helping him forget his worries. Millie, looking animated on the stool, clutches Chillin' her ventriloquist dummy on her lap. When I said Hank's name, I didn't miss the suspicion clouding Millie's face. I should tell her *I have no interest. In Hank or anyone else here. Nothing in this town interests me.* Instead, I decide to let her sweat it out.

Hank calls back. "Hey, Janelle."

"Hey there Hank." Again. To rattle Millie more. I'm feeling edgy and fried; who needs shit from Millie?

Finally, I say, "Hi Millie." Her mouth is down at the corners and she's fussing with Chillin's black nylon hair. Is Millie scheming to be Mrs. Hank number 2?

"Janelle, you look tired," Hank says.

Hearing it this way, with true sincerity, makes me sag further. I feel like a rag doll whose stuffing is showing at the seams. At least my shoe seam. "I guess I am a bit tired."

"I heard about Sly," he says.

"I'm very tired, too." Millie is not looking at all tired.

"You've got the stool," I say.

"You should know." She thumps on her wooden leg.

Plenty of mileage has come out of that leg. People feeling sorry have dumped serious money on Millie. She could get a newer lighter model made of aluminum. But, then what? I've heard different versions of the accident: a sawmill malfunction; a car jack come loose while she changed a truck tire; a couple more. Nobody knows for sure how she lost that leg from the knee down.

But Millie's rolling now. "And what with havin' to drag Chillin' around all the time! She's not exactly light you know."

Hank and I exchange looks. "Now, now, Millie," he says, "she can't be all that heavy being she's made out of a soft wood. I'm sure Chillin' wouldn't mind spending some time alone at home now and again."

"I *would* mind!" screeches the dummy suddenly coming to life.

He puts up a hand. "OK, OK. Everybody stay calm."

Chillin's head slumps onto her chest. "You've upset her," says Millie. "She feels her disability every moment of every single day. Of course, you two wouldn't know."

Ah, jeez, here it comes…

"The way *we* all do, those of us who happen to be physically challenged."

At this point I decide it's best to move along. I switch my sack purse to my other shoulder. Both feel sore. She should know what it feels like lugging a sack purse around in this heat, all day, while trying to figure out the next portion of your life. From what I heard she owns a car and rents a big apartment in a two-family house with a wraparound porch.

"You have a nice day," I tell her. "Chillin' too. Y'all both have a real good day. You, too, Hank. Bye for now."

"Bye, Janelle," he says softly.

CHAPTER 3

This two-roomer I rent near the swamp came furnished. The newspaper ad didn't specify. In the living room / kitchen I peel down to my underpants, sweating like I've been hosed. From the very day I moved here the auto-position crank on the Barcalounger didn't work. I have to hand crank into position. Flat out on my back I stare up at water staining the drop ceiling brown in places. This roof! Visions of hurricanes dance through my sleep.

Besides the Barcalounger, it also came furnished with a fake wood coffee table, 1950's style, a teensy-tiny really old TV on a stand, and one floor lamp. A single bed in the narrow bedroom. *Living room with flow* the newspaper ad read. It didn't mention a hundred year old mattress on metal springs. The ad made it sound sort of sweet and gracious. *Flow.*

It flows right into a makeshift triangular kitchen stuck in a corner of the living room. Stove, sink, a few cabinets slapped in. The fridge faces out on the room. Convenient for someone who wants their beer quick. Beige speckled lino flooring flows on into the bedroom with its one small window. A sweat box—the whole damn place. Every time I come in here, I'm suicidal.

There's not a single picture on these desert-sand walls. The empty paint cans were left out back—should I find a need to touch-up said the realtor lady who also said *desert-sand is trending.*

I suppose I could hang something. Even a calendar in the kitchen area. But, now? Jobless? One foot out the door?

I wiggle off the sticky vinyl Barca to get a bath towel to spread under myself. This airless dump could *scorch the hand of God.* Mama was fond of such expressions; when the deep heat of summer folded us into living corpses. But she's gone now and I'm no longer a kid. I picture Brother Sly living out his time in a cold refreshing place like Canada.

"Mama I quit my job," I say into the room.

CHAPTER 4

Persistent banging on the door shakes me out of a half-slumber. Mama doesn't bang her appearance but speaks softly. Clyde? I sure hope not Clyde.

I get up slowly, exhausted, pulling on my clothes, tip-toeing toward the door. Bending to peep through the mail slot. I know those ugly hairy legs. Mel. What does he want?

I say through the slot, "Yes?"

"Janelle we need to talk."

I count to ten. "I have to find my shoes."

We need to talk? Has he turned into my ex? Does he think I ripped him off? Stole a few Confederate capes from his barber shop? I slip my shoes on then open the door. The sun ratcheting through a sky so psychedelic blue it startles me into wakefulness.

Mel is batting away mosquitoes. "Can we at least move into the shade?"

I start toward the big Magnolia in full leaf. "This is the best shade I've got." Maybe he's found Sly or something to do with his whereabouts. "Is this regarding Sly?"

"No, no. Nothin' about him." He's batting at

mosquitoes around his ankles now. "Damn. You got a helluva mosquito problem here."

Duh, yeah! "Nile Fever proportions." I look up in the tree. A Cicada hangs dead off a leaf. Death. Everywhere. The world is coming down around us. "What do you want Mel?"

"The thing is, see, I don't like leaving things undone." Now he's batting around his face. "You and me, we made a good team."

I say nothing.

"Do ya think we could go inside a minute to get away from these critters?"

"I'm afraid my house is in disorder at the moment." He should know I practically bathe in OFF spray.

He puts out his hand. A hand that's empty. If he really meant what he said he could've palmed me a hundred for the sake of good will.

I just stare at him with my eyebrows raised. So be a jerk, I'm thinking.

"I don't see why we can't shake hands and start over," he says.

Start what over? Mel's hand still hanging out there.

"You see, the thing is, Mel—I'm plain tired of cutting

nails." And putting up with assholes. "It's a bad time for the world."

He shrugs. "The world is the world."

"That's the whole problem here."

"The world isn't the world?"

Round wet circles darken the arm pits of his pale-blue polo shirt. The little horse and rider stitched on. "Is that an official Polo shirt?" I ask him.

"Official?"

"Did you buy it off TV when they sell that stuff at discount 'cause it's fake?"

He shifts his weight. If that shirt is the real deal it had to cost him eighty-five plus.

"As a matter of fact I bought it in Miami Beach."

"Hm." I'm nodding. "So you shop on vacation in Miami Beach and pay me less than a day laborer."

"Now, look here."

"No, you look. Look around, Mel. I'm living in this shithole. I can't exist on what you pay it's that simple."

From the mosquitos he's starting to flip—batting and sputtering, saying, "I had this idea of installin' a wide screen in the shop. This way when we're slow, you can relax and watch a little TV."

"How does that pay my bills, Mel?"

He pulls up taller and straighter despite the mosquitoes; as if he has a higher position in life.

"This here... *place*—where you're livin' Janelle, happens to be an old chicken house."

"What!!!"

"That's right. Converted. Billy come up with the idea when he gave up the hens. I'm done messin' around. You comin' back to work or what?"

"Not at your pay scale."

"All right, then. Look around, you might find yourself a leftover egg or two."

"You knew all along and didn't warn me off rentin' this place?"

"I know everything. Where you choose to live Janelle just ain't my business." He puffs out his chest and the little horse and rider make a quick gallop.

CHAPTER 5

Back inside my *converted chicken house* I almost start crying. But I don't. Because I start worrying and that starts me calculating things. Mel could have me blacklisted all over town. Who will rent to me then? I'll have to move to another town. I don't have the kind of money required for a security deposit on a real apartment. In fact, I don't have much money at all. Tops, a few hundred. How can you save a dime when you're in the flamin' red at the end of each month? Bills come you throw half in the trash. Guaranteed they'll come back like homing pigeons.

I grab an apple from the fridge kicking the door closed. The fridge wobbles. How long before that hunk of junk gives up the ghost? It looks third-hand like it came from Cowboy Joe. Hundreds of plumbing appliances sitting in the tall weeds outside his shack. So many used toilets. Pretty gross. Not to mention the sinks, fridges, stoves, washers and dryers. Whatever Cowboy Joe can pick up dirt cheap or even free when a house becomes deserted. What a life, I'm thinking, gathering up other peoples' filth. Everyone knows that stuff isn't scoured down with AJAX. Like when my Grandaddy couldn't hold his bowels anymore. No matter how much they hosed off his undies, confronting the washing machine was a frightening event. This fridge—I wouldn't be at all surprised if it came off Cowboy Joe's lot. "Don't think about it," I say twirling the apple by the stem.

Munching, I contemplate my future. If there is one. Mel's got possible mob connections. In those movies there's always a barber shop scene. Often there's a murder in the barber shop, a big bloody shoot out. Afterward, the ones who aren't dead on the floor go out for a spaghetti dinner. In Mel's case, it would be fried fish. Down on my knees, clipping clipping clipping those toenails, Mel's true nature never quite dawned on me.

I get off the Barca moving around the room sniffing in corners. Smells tend to stick in the corners. No old chickens that I can smell.

CHAPTER 6

After washing up in my shower stall—the size of an old wooden phone booth—I put on my pink shorts with the turquoise flamingos and a white T. My sparkly flip-flops. Hair snapped back in a pony and long silver earrings studded with fake turquoise. Feels almost like celebrating my independence. Almost.

Taking the back roads it's a quick bike ride to town. The street lights are starting to flicker on, block by block. Not one big flash. This town being too cheap to update to a central grid. I place the old Schwinn on its side in high grass. The kickstand long rusted off, I suspect. This bike being part of my *home furnishings*. Then smoothing my shorts, I make my way toward Bingo's outdoor patio area behind the flat cement building.

Real bamboo surrounding two sides of the patio has grown taller than some Maples. Bingo planted it when he got home from Vietnam. He says it's planted to honor both sides. Of course, with him being real ancient now, his two sons run the place. Out here on the patio mainly it's beer and liquor and burgers. Fancier food inside. On

Memorial Day and Veterans' Day old Bingo makes an appearance at cocktail hour. It's sobering to see the old veteran in his army uniform. People make toasts in his honor. A somber scene, for sure. Then they play God Bless America through speakers and everyone joins in.

"I'd have to be starving for a month," I mutter; thinking of Mel's offer that we make up, business as usual.

"You been starving for a month?" It's Stevie-J local body builder gone big time TV talent. Grinning at me. "You don't look starved, Janelle. By the way I'm liking those shorts, very sweet."

Again with the sweet! What is it with the men in this town? Earlier it was Bucky Fuller. I manage a tight smile. You like them Stevie-J? Or you'd like to get in them? "Oh, gee, thanks."

According to local gossip Stevie-J wrestled an alligator. Supposedly. Then the story got changed to a crocodile. We don't have any crocs around here that I'm aware of. At any rate, they put up a big billboard over the interstate bridge. Stevie-J holding the creature high above his head. From down below, it's hard to get a true read on the actual species. It could have been an iguana.

Anyway, he banked a ton of money off that scheme and became fabulously famous. Drives a magenta Corvette with that special paint that glistens. He drives it really fast taking the turns in tight squares.

"Are you hip to hang with me?" he says.

"Why not."

"Don't trip over your excitement, Janelle."

"I can't stay long. This heat is knocking me to shreds."

"You need to turn up your A/C full blast. This is death weather."

Tell me about it. I walked around all day in death weather. I guess he's not aware I live in the chicken house. The A/C there is Model T. Complete with the rust of decades. Weakest possible air flow running tepid. Well, fuck it. Stevie-J was just a poor guy once upon a time. A poor guy with muscles to spare and a scheme that took him onto the TV talk show circuit.

"Was it really a croc?"

He smiles mysteriously. Then pushing me by my elbow we're on the patio, part of the growing gathering. "What are you drinkin', Janelle?"

"Gin ice lemon."

"Stay right here," he says pointing at the patio floor.

I feel sort of pinned. A few girls I know are here and I lift my hand to wave but they seem to look through me then disappear. Mel springs into my mind. Has he already started spreading his smear campaign? Thugs in the night with piano wire? The Klan? I heard they don't discriminate now. I start to shiver. In a little while at Karaoke time it's going to be total madness.

Stevie-J is back with the booze. "Janelle, how can you be shiverin' when it's like 110 in the shade?" He hands me the drink.

"I'm not cold, I just thought of something." My flip-flop catches on a piece of dry leaf. I scrape my foot against the patio to loosen it.

"Cool sandals," he says. "All that glitters." He clinks his beer against my glass.

"Hey, Stevie-J!" Someone screaming over the patio racket, "how's it hanging?"

"That's the new fry cook," he tells me.

I turn and see a guy in a stupid paper hat hanging out of Bingo's kitchen window.

"The fry cook," he tells me, grinning. "Not bad," he yells back, "how 'bout you?"

"Can't complain. Rassle any crocodiles lately?"

I watch for Stevie-J's reaction but he's dry as a tack.

"Don't want to press my luck," he shouts back.

The fry guy gives him two thumbs up and pulls his head inside.

I need a scheme. A scheme that will make me rich. I don't want to go down in history as the local girl who lived in the chicken house. These days, what with the virus, you can go down faster than you stand up. All around town they're dropping like flies. Most people in these parts think a fly swatter is the solution.

"Janelle?"

"Sorry. I was daydreaming."

Three girls who look jail bait stroll by squealing *Stevie-J*. The blonde flashes her tits. Nothing spectacular. "Seen better, seen worse," he says into my ear. Is that a lie out of consideration towards me? 'Cause mine are actually nothing to sneeze at.

We make some small talk. Soon the tiny white twinkle lights twisted through the bamboo flicker on making the patio almost magical. I mention to Stevie-J that I quit Mel's.

"I heard about that," he says.

He *heard.* No grass growing under Mel's big flap. I sip my drink thinking all in all I find Stevie-J a tad boring. He reminds me somewhat of the guys who come into Mel's. Younger. But the same rap tap.

"Where do you get your hair cut?" It's all I can come up with.

"I got a boutique barber comes twice a week to my house."

The line of all guitar pickers is starting to tune. Eight in a line all wearing cowboy hats. "You mean to say the barber goes straight to your house?"

"You don't think I'd hump on over to Mel."

I lick my lips even though they're not dry. "I don't expect you would, Stevie-J. Being that you're famous and all." I'm watching the pickers. "Why is it always all guitars?" Someone bumps me, sloshing my drink. It manages to miss my shorts and T-shirt just barely.

"Janelle, you 'bout ready for a refill?" He's grinning again. "If those aren't the cutest damn shorts. What are those birds, anyways, peacocks?"

"Flamingos." Hm. He doesn't know a flamingo from a peacock. Maybe he doesn't know a croc from an alligator from an iguana. "Almost ready," I tell him.

Most of the ice has melted. Obedient as a little lamb I down what's left in my glass.

CHAPTER 7

The pickers start their first tune. They do about five, sometimes more. Ten is their imposed limit. It depends on the crowd reaction. Luke warm tonight. The pickers keep it on the shorter side. Everyone seems to know exactly how to play their own game. What the hell is my problem?

"I'm glad that's over with," I tell Stevie-J.

I always think a horn or electric piano would add a dash of excitement to the pickers act before opening to the Karaoke. But the pickers do it their way. People are pretty much sloshed and hardly react anyhow. As far as I'm concerned, the best thing here is the towering bamboo. I'd like to see a monkey swinging branch by branch through the twinkle lights.

Not even an hour gone by and already I've run out of conversation. Stevie-J looking into my glass from time to time. That gets me to feeling jittery. I slow my sipping way down and decide not to let him buy me another drink. Who knows what's up his sleeve?

"OK, Janelle," says Stevie-J.

So deep in thought I didn't realize the pickers were done and packing up. "OK what?"

"I know you sing like an angel." He tickles me under the chin. "You gonna gift us with yer vocal talents tonight?"

Now that is the last thing I feel like doing. I'm dead tired from the day, and now these drinks. I feel drowsy rather than relaxed. "Stevie-J, that's real nice of you to suggest but honest to Pete I don't have one ounce of singing energy left in my entire body."

"You're a natural," he says. "One tiny little song is all I'm askin' of ya."

Oh good god almighty. Not to mention I feel a pee coming on. It will be packed with women in that two stall Ladies Room. Not to mention the long line to get in that snakes past the kitchen.

"Stevie-J, I need to powder my nose. And The Ladies' will be overflowin' with other women wantin' to do the same." Putting on a bit more *southern* can only help my case.

He takes the drink from my hand and sets it on the fake rock ledge. Other people had the same idea and so far no one has cleared away the empties.

"Janelle," he says with a wide grin, "being famous has its perks." And he sort of tugs me toward the restaurant which I'm not exactly keen on entering. A lot of these dodo birds have not been vaxxed. The whole idea of being jammed inside the building with a crowd is making me weak in the knees.

"Wait! Wait!" He stops to look at me. "I have to ask you a question, Stevie-J. Have you gotten the jab yet?"

"No, Janelle."

"In that case…"

"Hon. Do I look dumb to you? Do I run around all day saying *Praise the Lord*. Is that how you see me?"

I don't know how I see him. I shrug mumbling, "I don't know." Stevie-J is plainly not satisfied by this answer.

"Does a dumb person make all the money I made and get real famous so fast?" When I just shrug again, he says, "Don't trouble your sweet mind. I got my boost. I ain't messin' around with Mother Nature."

Mother Nature. I never quite thought of it that way. Still, I feel unsure. Men will say anything to get what they want. "Is that the absolute positive truth, Stevie-J? Do you swear on your Daddy's grave?"

Despite his Daddy being dead since the last decade I can see him taking this seriously. "Janelle, I swear."

His mouth seems to soften around the edges. "Now will you let me take you to the private bathroom? That only old man Bingo uses and only on military holidays."

That does sound impressive. The private bathroom. I'm wondering if old man Bingo has some cleanliness issues or it's just a thing his sons thought up. A way of showing their Daddy some real deep respect.

I let Stevie-J take my arm again, leading me around the side of the restaurant, then on into a type of wide hallway stacked with boxes. "What's this?"

"They use it for deliveries. You won't find any delivery guys here at this hour. C'mon. You're safe."

The gray cement walls radiate coolness. I want to stop and place my forehead against the wall. The cool might clear out some of the cobwebs that built up.

Stevie-J points to a door marked *Storage*. "Go on in, it's never locked."

Tentatively I open the door. This bathroom is a one shot deal. Single toilet, sink and urinal. It even has paper towels and pink soap in a dispenser. I take my time in the cool aloneness. If I linger, will Stevie-J get tired of waiting for me? Done his good deed and now has left the building? Like they said about Elvis back in the dark ages: *Elvis has left the building.* Mama was a huge fan.

"Everything OK in there?" Oh! He didn't leave the building.

"Uh huh," I shout through the door. "Like you said. Private. Very clean." I could stay here all night. "And cool. It's nice and cool in here."

"Well, good then. 'Cause now you owe me a song."

I open the door and step out. "I don't know what to sing."

"*Unchained Melody.*"

"You want *Unchained Melody?*"

"I heard you sing it one time and dropped to my knees."

CHAPTER 8

After two more gins he insisted on I'm pretty relaxed. Rubbery. A few times I even laugh when Stevie-J cracks some dumb joke. Then Mel arrives with a few of his cronies, all bluster and back slapping, and I'm not even affected. That's the thing about small towns—you really can't get away. Sly is gone but I'll bet he's always got this or that old situation flipping through his brain. You can be far away and still go crazy. It all depends how far your ghosts are willing to travel.

"Were you afraid when you wrestled the croc?"

Stevie-J ponders this. Or maybe by now he's good at coming up with fake answers. Suppose he actually did wrestle some large dangerous beast? Or is it all the booze making me less suspicious?

"Only afterward," he says. "During the tussle there was no time to be scared."

I'm nodding taking this in: *no time to be scared.*

"Now you wait right here Janelle while I check your place on the sign-in sheet."

The very moment he leaves me, Mel is here like a heat panting dog. "Janelle, you singin' tonight?"

"I don't know, Mel."

"You could tap dance instead," he says all twinkly eyed.

"That's real funny."

Stevie-J returns with yet another gin. I start to laugh. "Five and I'll fall on my face."

None of this is lost on Mel. He's squinting, less jolly now, his eyes sliding from me to Stevie-J. He's taking in Stevie-J's sharp haircut, he's taking me in. I'm not exactly coming across like some poor relation you throw dimes at. Mel is wondering. Well, let him.

"Have a good evening." Mel sounds frosty. Neither of us return the courtesy.

Up at the podium, Fred Fred, the local deejay, is announcing my name and the song. A big round of applause goes up and there's even some hooting and whistling.

"Oh, no! You made me go first Stevie-J?"

He gives me an affectionate little push. "Go get 'em."

Feeling light-headed I stumble through the crowd toward the Karaoke.

Fred Fred pecks me on the cheek. His standard bit for the ladies who sing. He has to reach his head up, since he's shorter than me. He covers his top hair comb-over with his signature gray fedora.

He starts clapping and the audience follows. "You tasty morsel," he says into the mic. His warm up banter that he calls *foreplay*. He can get pretty rank. He better not try with me.

"So, Janelle, you been singin' your whole life, ain't that the truth?"

He knows it's the truth. He probably shook my baby rattle in the carriage. "Sure, Fred. If you say so."

There's some snickering.

"Who's your favorite male singer?" He winks broadly at the audience. "If I may get a little personal here."

"The one who gives good head," someone yells.

"No argument there." Fred bows to his audience.

I can't stand his whole stupid bit that's already out of control. "As a matter of fact, Fred, I just adore all the singers out there pourin' their hearts out."

He tugs on the brim of his hat but he's pissed all the same.

"That's mighty liberal of you, Missy." *Liberal.* The dirtiest word you can use in these parts. I'm being harpooned.

There's some jeering from the crowd.

I can see Stevie-J muscling through to get nearer to me. I'm not afraid, but all the same it's nice to know there's some protection when it might be called for.

"Hit it, Fred Fred," I say.

Mumbling what sounds like *bitch*, little nasty man retreats behind his sound board. The music comes up.

I jump it, hot and liquid, spoon out *Unchained Melody* for all I'm worth.

CHAPTER 9

Stevie-J lifts my bike out of the weeds and chucks it in the rear of his silver pickup. I'm a little disappointed. I kind of expected the magenta Corvette. As he's telling me that I have star quality, I step onto the wide footboard and slide in. At least the black seat is real leather with that great smell. "That's sure nice to hear, Stevie-J, but right now what I need is a job."

"What are your qualifications?" He's lighting a joint.

"Such as?"

"Like what can you offer to the workplace?"

He's pumped the A/C to high and lowers all the windows. Sweet honeysuckle growing wild drifts in. The best time of day. Sun's been swallowed up, the crazy heat sinking into the ground. I picture it as going straight down to hell adding more heat to what are claimed to be unimaginably torturous temperatures. Worse than the chicken house? The priest claims the devil and his monsters cook up their schemes in a huge black cauldron that could feed a starving continent. I've heard those tales all my life. I don't quite take them literally. Despite his bad deeds, I don't picture Sly down there either.

Stevie-J offers me a hit. "Thanks but I'm going the squeaky clean route. It might help my karma to give up eating animals and smoking dope."

He's staring like I'm speaking a foreign language. The truth is—I'm not about to share spit during this health crisis. I read in Mel's newspaper that during the AIDS crisis lots of people lied to get laid. AIDS put my daddy in the ground from a blood transfusion. I was just a little girl.

"My karma feels so flat," I say. Even saying it comes out flat. The truth of me. "I have no particular skills. I have nothing to offer to the job market."

For sure I don't see myself wrestling large amphibious creatures.

"C'mon, Janelle. You just knocked about a hundred people off that patio. Man, nobody sings like you do. Meantime this pot is giving me extreme munchies. You wanna go to the fairgrounds and get some junk food? Ride the Ferris Wheel?" He leans in putting an arm across the top of my seat. "Huh? What would *you* like to do?"

I'd bet good money right now he has a major hard-on.

"I think the fairgrounds could be OK." I don't mention I was there earlier and am fair-grounded out of my skull. Plus, I'm not keen on running into Hank while I'm obviously with Stevie-J at the moment. It's good to keep your options open. "Maybe we could drive to Shrenksville, instead, and have some pub food?"

"Nah. Let's just do the fairgrounds and take things from there," he says.

What things?

Even though I've had my fill of the fairgrounds, I have to admit it is pretty all lit up against the night sky. At the ice cream stand I order a cone, double vanilla and chocolate. Owen asks through the open window if I want the chocolate drizzle, too.

"No thanks." All the same it was nice of him to ask. "Maybe next time," I say. If you look past the gap-tooth grin he's not bad. Bright blue eyes and blondish-brown hair, a slight brogue. He certainly has the charm. I say, "Luck of the Irish?"

He pounds the counter laughing. "I'm making your cone extra tall," he tells me. "And what's your flavor, Stevie-J?"

Used to being the center of attention, Stevie-J seems a bit off. Or maybe it's from the weed. "When you're done flirting… I'll have a waffle with all three flavors," he says.

Well that's fairly childish, I'm thinking. Owen moves away to fill the order. "I wouldn't exactly call that flirting," I say. "Just friendliness."

Stevie-J looks over the top of my head like I'm not here. Neither of us speaks. Owen is back in a jiffy. He passes my cone out the window.

"Wow, it is a mile high," I say. "Thanks, Owen. Now don't you go on getting in trouble on my account."

"Janelle he owns the damn place."

"Oh!"

"I'm toasting up your waffle golden," he tells Stevie-J. "Just be a minute."

"What-ever."

Ignoring the sour reply, Owen smiles at me. I wonder if all the men from his country are so gentlemanly.

Stevie-J's waffle and ice cream combo comes out on a square cardboard tray. "Let's sit down and eat," he says. "I feel bushed."

"Bye, Owen," I say.

We stroll toward some empty benches. My cone dripping faster than I can keep up with licking it. "I shoulda taken extra napkins." Just as I sit, a blob of ice cream hits the ground.

"He keeps that ice cream freezer too damn low. That's why it's meltin' so fast. Mine, too." Disgusted, Stevie-J stands up tossing the waffle in a wire trash bin.

"Ohhhh…"

"What?"

I don't say the rats are gonna feast, or that I would've eaten it melting or otherwise. "Didn't your mama teach you about throwing away good food and all the starving children of the world?"

"She taught me nothin' much. That matters."

I'm licking the cone as fast as possible. "You know, for some reason I thought a totally different man owned the ice cream serve."

"Yeah, totally different. Lee."

"But you just said Owen …?"

"Best not to discuss it right now. Eat your cone before the whole thing falls to the ground. We're here to have a good time. Ain't that right, Janelle?"

"I guess so." I can't eat fast enough to stop the drips.

"Is piano wire made from cat guts?"

"Now there's a strange question."

"You know, if these fairgrounds were set beside an ocean, say—a wide ocean that stretched to a horizon line, this could be quite an amazing place." Then I suck out the last of the ice cream from a pin hole I bit in the bottom of the sugar cone.

CHAPTER 10

It appears Stevie-J and I have two different mindsets on how to end the evening.

"I don't think so," I say, squirming out of his grasp.

We're parked outside the chicken house that's pitch dark inside and out, which makes it hard to see that it's a chicken house.

"I've had a really long day and I need to go to sleep now, Stevie-J."

"You live here in the chicken house?" He's reaching for me again.

So he knows it's a chicken house. I suspect if he knows the whole damn town knows. Mel was trying to snooker me. "I only come here for spa vacations."

"I remember this place as a kid," Stevie-J is saying. "A bad thing happened here."

Ah, jeez. Just what I don't need to hear. More bad surrounding me. I need some clean clear space if I'm ever going to start over.

I open the heavy truck door and get out. I hear Stevie-J's loud groan, then he turns on the truck lights and he gets out, too, around the front to my side. Already the mosquitoes have found us, he's whacking the air with his hand. Under these circumstances the cicada and cricket racket isn't at all soothing.

"Don't you want to know what happened here?" he says.

"Not while I'm being chewed alive."

"We could take the story inside."

"Not tonight, Stevie-J."

"You're livin' in a place with some serious history and you got no interest?"

He sort of groans again. Well, somewhere between a moan and a groan. "You know what, Janelle, you are seriously confusing. Can't say I ever met a chick like you."

Was that intentional? A *chick* who lives in a chicken house? And I don't want to be confusing. Not now, or maybe ever. I don't know what I want, but I know it doesn't exist between those thin walls where I'm living. Or anywhere else in this swampy, miserable town. Today I thought Kenny Rogers could make me a little bit happy. Chicken and biscuits and gravy. "Well, Stevie-J, you put the truck lights on which brings the bugs."

"It's real quiet here," he says making a joke.

"Thanks for a fun night. I'm going in now."

"All by your little lonesome?"

"You would hate it in the chicken house."

"I can put up with a lot more than folks think."

He runs his finger down my arm so lightly I can't be sure it wasn't a bug that touched down.

The moment the door opens I smell dampness. I can hear Stevie-J cranking the truck engine. In here dampness reigns, and the mold of a thousand lifetimes. Chicken lifetimes, that is. I'm sure some other folks have had the bad luck to call this place home. For a second I almost run outside and yell *wait!* Something stops me. If I leave with him it's like I've given in and become his little whore. I listen to the truck grinding as he drives off.

I stand in the middle of the room. Probably should have gone with him. I'm always sad when I'm here. I feel it somewhere in my chest—a tightening and swishing. I'm having second thoughts about the barbershop. The work was totally gross, but it was a place I had to be every day. I suppose I could always find work at the fairgrounds. In the blistering heat and tropical downpours. I suppose.

Thoughts of kicking around the fairgrounds all day stir me up and I sit on the edge of the Barca and feel the tears start to well. Tracks of my tears. *See, you could be a professional singer,* Mama is saying, *there's always a song in your heart.*

The very day I moved in here a few of the vinyl buttons were missing from the Barcalounger. The little buttonholes have bits of yellow string hanging from the tufts. I roll a piece between my fingers. If I stay on too long here my own strings are gonna pop.

Standing up, I circle the place counting: one Mississippi, two Mississippi, three Mississippi—doesn't take much to get back to the starting point at nine Mississippi. What is *my* true starting point? Singer? With the virus still hanging in the air, becoming a singer seems pretty hopeless. I suppose I'd have to travel to Nashville. Hang around there getting myself dug in to that scene. I don't see it happening.

I sit down again then get right back up. Putting my face close to the A/C and whispering a little air prayer. "Please God in your intense wisdom make this air cold. One Mississippi, two Mississippi..." Useless. It blows the same—weak and murky.

Janelle, go platinum.

Now what??? Does Mama mean my hair? Or is she yakking about a platinum record?

Everyone in my family has an opinion and more than glad to share it. Take my sister, Raelyn, living somewhere off Spain these last few years. When Mama was alive I'd get the updates: Raelyn on an island in a villa where flowers grow up the sides of white houses and the sand is black. The inhabitants survive off tiny morsels called Tapas that are way overpriced, and they eat far into the night, along with a lot of wine. My family—always went for the extreme. Raelyn, she'd eat grass if it kept her weight down. She'd also freakin' croak to find out I'm living in a chicken house. Now take Chillin' Millie. I'll bet when she's feeling alone, she pulls the dummy's strings, or however that dummy works, and Chillin' springs to life.

Tomorrow I'm going to buy myself a plant. Possibly red. And maybe even white-wash these desert-sand walls that are slowly burying me alive.

CHAPTER 12

I wake up in the murk of the half dead. I sure didn't sleep like the dead. More like a ghost on patrol duty. Everyone living in a twenty mile span of here made an appearance in my dreams. People I like and those I despise. Yak-yaking, complaining, laughing, flying over the swamps, screwing with abandon. At one point Stevie-J held a knife to an alligator's throat demanding allegiance.

I wake up in a sweat. So what else is new. It's time to make tracks out of here. Screw the whole white-washed walls idea. This will always be a chicken house. I may just be the biggest chicken yet to inhabit this dump.

Stop yer bitchin' all the time.

Mama? *Somebody* has a point.

In the tight stall I shower and shampoo quickly. The floor always floods 'cause the door doesn't close tight. I twist my wet hair into a knot, throw on yellow shorts and a black T. My new black Skechers from HSN which are kind of adorable. Somehow, I can think better when I'm clean. I'll go to the diner for breakfast. I can figure things out over a second coffee.

Just as I'm getting on the bike, a magenta Corvette, low and sleek, slides onto my land. Oh, boy. Well, it's not exactly my land. But I do pay rent so for now... Stevie-J toots the horn a few times. One toot would be enough, I'm thinking, shading my eyes from the sun illuminating the sparkles in the paint job.

He sticks his head out the window. "Where you off to?"

"Thought I'd go on over to The Bluebell for pancakes."

"Hop in," he says.

Hesitating, I straddle the bike.

"Now what?" he says.

I place the bike in the weeds and walk toward his window. Steve-J saying, "I shoulda called first but I don't have yer number."

"That's 'cause I don't have one."

"Wha?" His eyes widen as he takes this in. "Everybody's got a number."

"Not me."

Stevie-J's dark hair is spiked in a new style. I'm thinking about all the gray heads Mel cuts, how they all come out looking the same. Thin on top, or bald, with way too long sideburns. Sometimes those scissors going *clip clip clip clip* were enough to drive me out of my mind.

"Pancakes. Hop in," he says.

I sink into the low-slung black leather seat with its bubbly grains under my bare legs. So low down, it feels like I'm sitting on the road. "What's this leather called?"

"Dunno. Popcorn leather?"

"It's nice."

"Yeah. It was an add on."

I'm trying to compute the price of such a fancy sports car.

"This car cost a bundle," he says like reading my mind. That's all he says. He punches the radio on. "You know this song, Janelle?"

"I'm afraid I don't, Stevie-J. I don't know the religious songs at all. My family is devoutly atheist. Well… that is what's left of my family."

His head jerks. "You sayin' you don't believe in Jesus?"

If I tell the truth will he throw me out of his luxury wheels? "I don't know, I don't know what I believe. It's all a confusing mess, in my opinion. Why would Jesus let so many die from the virus? Even the little babies?"

For a couple of blocks Stevie-J doesn't answer. Is he considering where he's going to drop me off? Finally he says, "You have to take the word of the Lord as Gospel."

Frankly I don't even know what the hell that means. Mama being a practicing Buddhist kept us clear of all the god stuff. Toward the end she showed me a little altar with a fat jade Buddha kept on her closet shelf. *Real jade*, she said with pride. When she was on her death bed she told me to sell it but not for a penny less than five hundred. It took care of her cremation expense and the bronze jar.

At the one light in town Stevie-J has to stop. "I can't stand getting caught at the red light." He's gunning the engine. The car behind is tooting and shouting things to him, their heads hanging out the windows. He raises the volume on the radio, saying, "Don't look back at them heathens."

"How do you know they're heathens?" Another day of hot liquid sunshine. I could stay in this car until night, him driving us 'round and 'round, the ice cold air pumping. "What makes them heathens?"

"They don't practice The Word."

Last night at Bingo's, I wasn't aware of god anywhere on that patio. He must've been hiding out in the bamboo. In fact, Stevie-J led me to believe the exact opposite. "Ya know, last night you specifically said you didn't go around saying *Praise the Lord*."

Sensing a road block here, Stevie-J lets the topic die. Just as well. I look over and he smiles, and I smile, too. 'Cause what's the point in spoiling a big thick stack dripping maple syrup? A slab of crispy bacon. Really good coffee with Half & Half. My stomach is growling. The music blasting out of the Corvette's top of the line speaker system is covering that up, too.

CHAPTER 13

Naturally there's a line to get in The Bluebell. But people keep moving aside saying: *Go on in, Stevie-J, have your breakfast, gotta keep those muscles pumpin'.*

I can't help but notice they are also aware of me, walking in ahead of him, his hand resting on my shoulder. Busy putting their version of two and two together. Which pretty much annoys me. The gossip for today will be that he's doing me. By suppertime they'll have me pregnant, by morning in labor.

Darlene, who's been working here—like forever—lifts her eyebrows upon seeing me—before showing us to a big booth at a window. "This is nice," I say. "Being shaded and all." Darlene slaps down two sticky plastic menus, saying *two coffees* before sauntering away.

There's folks in here I've known practically forever plus some new and less than exciting looking additions. Working at Mel's all day had made me kind of hidden; like corn waiting to be shucked from the husk. Sort of made me feel invisible. Just Mel and his cronies, day in and day out. Now wouldn't you know it—the old devil himself planted beside our booth. He punches Stevie-J playfully on the shoulder. "No grass grows under your feet my good man," Mel says.

For the most part I've never seen Stevie-J look anything but friendly. Now a dark flatness crosses his eyes like the black holes in the universe. If you fall in you don't come out.

"What the hell you drivin' at Mel?" His tone catches Mel off guard; he kind of sways beside the booth then regains his balance.

"Why, Stevie-J, I was simply referrin' to the sharp new hair you're sportin'."

Yeah, Mel, right, I'm thinking. Not one of your ugly dated hair cuts. And I'm thinking these menus just get stickier and stickier. Someone should wipe them down. Could the virus attach to the muck on these menus?

Stevie-J opens his and begins reading the pancake choices out loud. Darlene puts down the two coffees. In here, steaming coffee is lovely, 'cause The Bluebell maintains frigid temps. Some people even have on sweaters. Darlene comes back a minute later with the silver creamer. Mel, being ignored, still stands here.

"That's Half & Half, right, Darlene?"

"Righto, Stevie-J." Treating him like her little pet lamb.

"Well," Mel is saying, "Y'all have a great day."

Neither of us looks up.

When we're finished with the menus Stevie-J locks hands with me across the table. "Janelle, would you describe yourself as a contented woman?"

"Contented? In what way contented?"

Darlene is back saying *Jimmy's busy so I'll take your order.*

I order a stack of buttermilk. Stevie-J orders the buckwheat. "Hon, not the buckwheat," she tells him. "That's yesterday's batter. Go with the buttermilk or the blueberry is fresh too."

"Make it blueberry," he says. "Thanks for the tip, Darlene."

"Any time, sugar!" Middle aged, wrinkly around the mouth, she'd have him in a heartbeat. So would practically every other woman in town. Stevie-J has those classic movie star good looks. Plus, there's all that big money now. I suspect some of the males around here wouldn't throw him out of bed either. Sly crosses my mind then slips away.

"Janelle," he says after his first sip of coffee, "I'm gonna help you get famous."

My first sip is still going down and I nearly choke.

CHAPTER 14

After breakfast we sit in his car having a meeting (his words). "But I don't want to be famous," I tell him. "I shouldn't have eaten the whole stack now I feel bloated."

"It's out of your hands, Janelle. Your future has been decided. You couldn't stop it if you tried. It's your karma."

Karma is a word Mama used to use. I really don't know how to take this in. Is Stevie-J one of those self-deluded people who think they know every answer to life? To *my future*? Just getting out of the chicken house would be huge enough for me. "I never had big plans," I tell him.

He rolls his eyes. "That's the problem."

For the first time I notice blue shadows under his dark eyes. If he'd been born with blue eyes and the blue shadows, he may have looked like a freak. His eyes are a warm chocolate color. It's the blue shadows that make him sexy and a little dangerous looking.

"Janelle, I'm going to teach you to think big."

"The first thing I have to do big is get to Mel's and collect the pay he owes me."

"Let's go," he says, the car moving forward. "But remember—big and necessity are two different cats."

Already I'm feeling exhausted; despite the cool air blowing and the incredible leather seat.

He drives to Mel's and pulls to the curb. "Tell him I've got the car running, so he better be quick about it."

I nod and step out. The heat hits me like a wall. I'm feeling a bit rocky from the heavy breakfast; plus going in and out twice from the ice cold car into the screaming heat. My feet not quite touching the ground. Some sort of weirdness is taking place.

Inside the shop Mel is bent over the shampoo sink. He sees me and smirks. "Change your mind?"

"You owe me a week's back pay."

"I know that. You think I was gonna cheat you out of your due?"

Dale Lynex, getting his head scrubbed, says, "Janelle, you do it so much nicer."

Mel splashes Dale's face with the hose and Dale jerks. Mel says *sorry* like he doesn't mean it.

"Stevie-J is waiting in the car so I'd like my pay after you rinse Dale."

"You want it now Janelle?" Shoving the hose into my hand. "You're in such a big hurry you rinse Dale."

Even though this sort of shocks me, I don't let on. "I'd be happy to rinse Dale."

"She gets part of the tip money," Dale says.

"Yeah. You can add it to my wages." All of a sudden I feel kind of bitchy. "I'll give you a nice cool rinse at the end," I tell Dale.

"Janelle, I swear," says Dale, "if you ever open a shop of your own…"

At the register, counting out my money, Mel lets out a honk.

"Dale I promise you'll be the first to know." Like I would want to be stuck in some barbershop ever again.

"Give Janelle a crisp tenner from me," he says to Mel.

In a huff now, Mel passes us in long strides to his 'office' at the back.

Out of earshot I say, "Dale would you like a free cream rinse?"

He laughs. "Why not!"

I finish him up and dry his head with a fresh towel. Not one of those used towels Mel lets dry out then re-folds and puts back on the shelf.

As I'm chatting with Dale, the Chinese wig guy comes in to collect the hair.

"Hi Mr. Wu."

He smiles and bows slightly. "Melville not here?"

"Oh he's here, all right. In his office."

"During daytime in office?"

Dale is sitting up now. "I'm dripping a little, Janelle."

"Sorry, Dale." I wipe off the back of his neck.

"Yeah, Mr. Wu, I know, it is unusual. But you see, I quit yesterday."

"You quit?" He looks confused, cradling his empty hair bag as if it were a baby. "Why wash hair then?"

"I'm just doing Mel a little last minute favor."

Mr. Wu looks more confused. "You quit but still work?" He sits in a customer chair with the hair bag on his lap. "Hot day," he says.

"They're always hot."

I take the comb from the blue Barbicide and slick back Dale's wet hair. Where the hell are my wages? I want to get out before Mel gets caught up with Mr. Wu on collecting the hair. They can spend upwards of an hour collecting, dividing by color and texture and condition, then haggling over price. Sly took care of the hair collection part of the business. Mel is on his own now. With everything. I stifle a laugh.

He finally comes out of his office empty handed. When I start to protest, he says, "Hold on, Janelle."

"I can't leave Stevie-J out there with the car idling."

"I think he can afford to waste some gas."

"That's not the point!"

Furious, I throw down the towel I used on Dale. "Is that a new towel?" Mel bends over snuffling the towel like those cartoon pigs hunting truffles.

"It's now or never, Mel." I don't even know what I mean. I feel so furious.

Mr. Wu speaks up. "You owe Janelle money she already work for?"

"Mr. Wu you need not trouble yerself," Mel says.

"No business with corrupt person." Mr. Wu stands up. "Business done."

"Oh for god almighty sakes!" Mel says.

Clutching the hair bag Mr. Wu leaves the shop.

Nobody speaks for a moment. Then Dale says, "You got some real entertainment going on in this here establishment."

In his fury, Mel turns the shade of a blood-red rose.

CHAPTER 15

Stevie-J walks in. "What's the hold up?"

"Oh, just my back pay."

"You saying he ain't payin' what he owes you?"

Mel is shaking hair off a wet towel. "Can y'all wait just a damned second!"

"I have been waiting and I'm still waiting," I say.

"Get her money, Mel."

Mel bellows: "Put a broom up my ass I'll sweep the floor too. I'm a one man band now that she's pulled out."

Stevie-J folds his arms jutting his head forward. Maybe he's debating about holding Mel up over his head like the croc. "Quit stallin' and pay the lady what she's owed."

Mel storms back to his office.

Stevie-J is tapping one cowboy boot. "I never seen anything quite like this. A woman does her work then her employer don't pay her? How does that add up to fair? I'm tempted to call in the law," he's saying, when Mel appears with a brown pay envelope.

"Count it out." He thrusts it at Stevie-J.

"Give it to Janelle, it's her money."

Mel hands me the pay envelope which he hasn't bothered to seal.

I take out the cash. "It's right," I say.

"You got my tenner?" says Dale.

"Yes, and thank you very much Dale."

"You got mold in here." Stevie-J is pointing at Mel. "Smelt it the minute I stepped in."

I'm picturing a dark horrible bearded mold that climbs the walls of flooded houses after hurricanes.

"C'mon," says Stevie-J taking me by the arm.

We hit the car laughing. "Is it true you could smell mold?"

"No, darlin'. Just giving him some of his own back."

CHAPTER 16

The price of pleasure is pain. I think it's in the scriptures. I think Sly may have made that comment from time to time. Because, soon, I will have to leave this incredible car that's so tight it's like a spaceship on wheels. With the non-stop cold air and incredible sound system and seats you could live in till you die.

Stevie-J interrupts my daydreaming. "Whatchu gonna do with all that money?"

"Very funny. It will hardly cover my rent."

"Why I thought you might treat me to a Berliner Weisse beer at the Rathskeller in Shrenksville."

"Um… I really need to be getting home soon."

"Janelle, you think I'd let you pay? I was just pullin' your chain. Your *Unchained Melody*. I never heard anyone sing it like you. Damn near took me apart. For a little girl you have a lotta power."

Pulling my chain on the beer. Well that's a relief, I guess. A few Berliner Weisse would empty out the pay envelope fast. "How do they make those drinks so sweet?" I say.

"They shoot a raspberry syrup into the beer. It's a German classic. Like you're a classic, Janelle."

There's knocking on my side window. "It's Mr. Wu!"

Stevie-J lowers the automatic window, leaning across me. "Hey, there, Mr. Wu. You in need of a little cooling off?"

Mr. Wu shoves his hand in. "Here, Janelle, you take card."

I look at the writing on the plain white card rubber-stamped: *Wu Enterprises*. Plus a phone number with an area code I don't recognize written in ink.

"You phone we talk business."

Kind of stunned, I just shake my head. Then Mr. Wu bows and he's gone.

I pass the card to Stevie-J. "What could he possibly want with me?"

He stares at it then hands it back, pulling away and leaving rubber at the curb. We move fast out of town and onto the interstate. The trees on both sides looking parched and about to fall over.

CHAPTER 17

When the famous billboard appears Stevie-J slows the car. I stare up hard but still can't make out the species of the creature he's holding above his head. However, I decide not to mention that. We're having a nice day; things have worked out; why spoil it by questioning the nature of the beast?

"I wonder what I could possibly offer Mr. Wu in the way of business?"

Nevertheless, it puts a bit of a bounce in my heart. Mr. Wu, a man of business, has decided I'm worth doing business with. Or some such thing.

"Stevie-J, I'm going to get fat hanging out with you. What else do you do besides breakfast, lunch and dinner?"

He smacks his knee and breaks out laughing. "You wanna drive?"

"What! You mean this car? This Corvette?"

"Why not?"

"Does it have a shift?"

"'Course. You can drive stick, right?"

"Yeah, I learned on stick. My daddy had a pickup. But I don't know, Stevie-J. What if I crash the Corvette?"

He's slowing down and moves the car onto the grassy shoulder. "I'll buy a new one. But you won't crash. You're not the type to crash a car. I'd bet money on it."

"You can tell how people drive by their types?"

"You can tell a lot about people just by the little clues they drop."

He's getting out. I wonder what my clues are? We switch places and I settle back in the driver seat. "Oh... this is so nice."

"You want the seat adjusted?" he says.

"Yeah. It's kind of a little far back for me, my legs being shorter than yours are."

"Yeah. I noticed your legs. Just push that lever on the side and it will spring forward or back. To where you want it."

I do it a couple of times then it feels right. Wow. I'm so in command in the driver seat. I haven't felt in command of anything... in, like, forever.

"Just start slow till you get the feel of her," he says.

So his car is a *her*. "Does her have a name?" I say teasingly.

"Cora. What else would you name a Corvette?"

The drive to Shrenksville is like nothing I've ever experienced. Most of my life I've bounced around in trucks that could dislodge vital organs. Cora is one smooth ride. Low to the ground and a wheel so tight I almost feel I'm a part of this beautiful machine. "In Cora you can forget your troubles."

"Sing Hallelujah c'mon get peppy…" he belts out.

There he goes with the hallelujah. But I don't say anything; though it's definitely sloshing around in my mind.

"Stevie-J, before you became so super rich, did you have your down days?"

"Never, princess. I don't let anything chew my spirit."

Oh, jeez. Spirit. Is that more of the god stuff again?

"How is Raelyn?" he says.

My sister. "I don't know. She lives in Spain. On an island. It has black sand."

I'm hoping that's enough to satisfy him.

"Does she have a man?"

"No. Raelyn is gay."

"Impossible!"

I sigh. Nobody ever believes Raelyn is gay. "Look,

I'm telling you. If you want to go to Spain and ask her for yourself well be my guest."

He seems somewhat shook by this information, and lights another joint. "Raelyn and I had some pretty famous romps. She must've turned gay from Spain."

"I don't think you turn gay from living in a certain place."

"Well she gave no indication."

I'm thinking this might be a good time to switch back to the passenger seat. "Stevie-J, if you were gay would you blast it to the treetops in a town like where we live?"

He takes a few hits. "I s'pose not." After a moment he says, "Nah. I still don't believe it."

"I think we should switch places," I tell him. The shoulder of the road is fairly flat at this stretch and traffic is light. It would be a good place for me to pull over.

"No! I want you to deliver us straight to Shrenksville."

Deliver like we're a loaf of bread?

He sits back smoking, turns up the sound, and honestly it's starting to get to my eyes, despite this great air cooling system; plus the volume at this level is distracting me. I sneeze a few times. And start feeling sad. I wasn't sad all day but now I'm sad. Lately the smallest thing can make me sad. Sly once said it's because I feel ungrounded. At least with Sly you could shoot the breeze in all honesty. Stevie-J being a whole other situation. Strings attached. Like Millie with Chillin'. Only I can't put him into a suitcase.

"Raelyn can't be gay," he's saying. "We had a baby together."

It's my turn to be stunned. I was just deciding where to park, under that thick tree or out in the open of the shoulder.

I think I screamed. Then I said, "Where is the baby?"

"It died. Two days after. Little tyke was premature. Never left his incubator. She never got to hold him."

A boy baby. He never left the incubator. My neck has gone rigid. How could Raelyn be even somewhat pregnant and no one notices? No, no, impossible. He's messing with my head. "Was he named before he died?"

"Raelyn named him. Aloysius. From that Italian saint. Little Al she meant to call him. Also, after your Uncle who got killed in Vietnam."

Little Al. For two days we had a baby in the family named Little Al. Who knew?

CHAPTER 18

My heart is pounding. We switch seats. Pretty much the rest of the drive to Shrenksville even the radio stays mum. I want to ask Stevie-J a million questions but what's the point? If I learn about Little Al's hair color, or that he was a bald baby, or find out his eye color, I will always carry him, too. Not the way Raelyn did, of course. But carrying a baby can mean a lot of different things. This information has taken the fizz off the day. I could never let Stevie-J lay a hand on me now.

"I will never believe Raelyn turned lesby," he says.

"Oh, Stevie-J! That's 'cause you don't want to. Trust me, she's a lesbian."

He parks the Corvette in the shaded part of a weedy lot behind The Rathskeller.

"Once I loved her," he says. "And she loved me."

"Things change."

Like today, for instance. It started out with stacks of pancakes and laughs and now it's practically a funeral. The death of Raelyn's sexual desire for him. Stevie-J looks truly pierced through the heart.

We drink too many Berliner Weisse. I get drunk. Not many people are here at lunch time. My glass is big and bulbous and they re-fill past half way each time it goes down. The wait-staff all wear these Germanic type outfits which are very corny but add to the general experience.

Stevie-J, who can hold his liquor, and then some, is looking kind of scattered. The news of Raelyn having taken a toll. What did he suppose she's been doing the past couple years in a foreign country? If not women, it would have been men. Is he OK with *that*? He must've been. 'Cause to my knowledge he never went running over there to bring her home.

He asks one of the younger waitresses her name.

"Brunhilde," says the girl. A blonde braid wrapping her entire head like bread loves at the German bakery. She's pretty in an old style German way, with big sturdy arms and bright natural flushed cheeks.

"You live around here?" he says to her.

"I live up top The Rathskeller," she says.

"Would that be the ground level, or up above that?" he says.

She looks confused, pointing one finger up. An applique flower on her fluffy-edged apron is drooping like it might come off. I want to tell the girl to ignore him, and that she needs to put a few stitches in that flower, and that maybe the other flowers need reinforcing, too. I want to tell Stevie-J to leave the girl out of things. What happened between him and Raelyn is ancient history.

"Will you be having any food?" the girl asks.

Suddenly my head feels filled with stones. "Maybe some food would be a good idea," I say.

She leaves and returns with the menus. Before I can even open mine, he tells her: "Sauerbraten and boiled potatoes. And the creamed spinach."

"I don't think I want to eat anything that heavy, Stevie-J."

"You might like a crisp schnitzel," the girl says to me. "It comes with wilted spinach on the side."

"That sounds very good."

She smiles and takes the menus away. With that, Stevie-J's head falls on the table like a big rock. Glasses, plates, everything flying off. A second later, he stands up, and before I can say a single word he collapses right across the table, bringing the whole thing down.

On me. Wait-staff come running. I'm starting to feel hysterical. I'm crying. Maybe he dropped dead. I can't even check because I'm stuck under this big round of plywood pressing into my legs. Stevie-J, having rolled off, has hit the ground flat on his back.

They're lifting the table off me. I'm soaked in beer and water. My legs feel bruised everywhere. Stevie-J is still on the floor, his eyes open staring up.

"Is he drunk?" says a man in a suit who I figure must be the manager or owner.

I don't know what to say.

"Should we call the ambulance service?" the man says.

I kneel next to Stevie-J. "Are you OK, can you hear me?"

"Raelyn?"

"It's Janelle."

I look up and tell the man in the suit, "He'll be OK. No ambulance is required."

They help him get on his feet. He sways a bit, and everyone goes *Ooooooohhhh*. Then he seems to stabilize and he just looks embarrassed and keeps saying he will pay for everything he wrecked.

CHAPTER 19

At the insistence of the man in charge, with Stevie-J objecting that he's *all right now*, I drive the Corvette back. *It could be his heart* the man in charge whispered to me. *You should know*, I thought, taking in his cold heartless expression. The car drives like a dream. All the way home Stevie-J never says a word.

After his admission about Raelyn, and all that went down, any thoughts of us together as a couple have vanished as quickly as Sly vanished.

By the time we hit Main Street the sun is sinking. Almost a repeat of the other night at Bingos—us together with the sun going down. Except this time I'm in the driver seat. Literally. Mr. Wu crosses my mind. What could he possibly want? I'd kind of dismissed the whole business card thing but now I think I might follow up. It can't be my hair he wants for a wig— nobody wants carrot colored hair with more kinks than waves. I feel something new on my horizon. The way elephants parched for drink in The Sahara can sense water hundreds of miles away.

"Tell you what, Janelle." He's been so quiet this startles me.

"How are you feeling, Stevie-J?"

"Drop me off at my place and take the Corvette home. You can bring it back tomorrow."

"You sure about that?" Seen driving alone, without him in this car, tongues are sure to wag.

"Yeah. I got the truck so I won't be without wheels."

"OK!"

"See little sister, I told ya I'm in yer court."

I glance over. He's grinning like the old Stevie-J.

"Where'd you learn to drive so good?" he says.

A boring tale about corn and day labor and a truck with bad tires. "I forget," I tell him.

"Well, anyways. You want to stay for a swim?"

I pull up his sloping driveway. His house is a beautiful thing. I've only seen it from the road. Lots of wood and glass. I did hear he put a pool in. People say a turquoise pool.

"I don't have my swim suit."

"Ya got two choices. Swim in yer shorts and top or without 'em."

A cool dip after this day. This day of days. Where's the harm? Plus it would keep me away from the chicken house longer. Plus, I have to admit I'm just dying to see inside his house. I'm sure Raelyn saw inside. Down to the last square inch. Then I think of the baby.

"I'll pass for this time, but thanks for the invite."

Stevie-J lets out a big laugh. "You ain't going swimmin' 'cause you're thinkin' about Raelyn. Am I right or am I right?"

"You're wrong."

"Well, I got some news for you Janelle. I was a poor dirt farmer when your sister knew me. In the biblical sense, that is."

A poor dirt farmer. That hadn't occurred to me. But it does make sense, time wise. Still, I decide not to. I tell him I have some grocery shopping to take care of.

"Good enough," he says, waving before going inside his incredible home.

CHAPTER 20

I have to move quickly unpacking the trunk to avoid the mosquitoes as much as possible. The hearty little shits manage to have a light meal off my legs anyway. My poor bruised legs and now the itchy bites.

I shove all the bags in the fridge, including the dry goods, for sorting tomorrow. My head feels on a tilt. Too much to take in for one day. The baby has totally blown my brains out. I wonder how Raelyn managed to keep that secret from Mama?

Raelyn can survive just about anything. She would've made a good soldier. It doesn't work like that for me. I can barely cope. I look like I'm coping 'cause I still have good looks. Well, except for all the bruising now but that's temporary. When things start to unravel, I start doing the same. We're sisters. You'd think I woulda picked up at least a few of her survival skills.

Janelle it's you driving a mighty expensive sports car.

"Mama not now please. I just want to crash."

I kick my Skechers into a corner. Though she does make a good point.

During sleep I sense a presence. It wakes me. I keep a tiny night light going. There's no one in the place. Still, I can't shake it off. I even sense a smell that's soft like peaches in a pile at the market. Then my body seems to take on that same peachy smell, which is odd since I'm sweaty and a mess from the table crashing down and all that. I was too damned beat to shower before bed. I do eventually fall back to sleep but it's restless and I wake up early.

Outside, the morning bugs are buzzing. Today feels a teensy bit cooler. Not so much as to make any real difference. My senses are on high alert. Every prick of sound and smell, the slightest breeze, I'm noticing. For some strange reason I've taken Mr. Wu's card outside. I stare at it in my hand. Nothing special about it. In fact if I didn't know his line of business, this card would tell me nothing.

Going back inside, I pour a bowl of Cornflakes from my shopping expedition drowning them in milk till they float. Suddenly I have this impulse to eat in the car. I grab the Corvette key, carrying the bowl of Cornflakes out, eating in the comfort of the lovely seat and super-cold air conditioning. The nicest breakfast I've had since moving to this dump. Lately I have this strong desire for milk. After devouring the Cornflakes, I drink from the bowl what milk is left. So far the fridge is holding. Fingers crossed. Fingers crossed. Fingers crossed. The psychic in Mel's newspaper said in order to cement a desire you must speak the primary emotion into the air three times in a row. The psychic called it *The rule of three.*

I suppose I will have to return Stevie-J's car at some point though I wouldn't mind keeping it forever.

Then there's Mr. Wu. Might as well get that out of the way, too. It's so mysterious. I go back inside, taking a swig from the cold Tropicana in the glass bottle and wonder what the hell is going to happen today.

Using almost all cold I shower quickly. When I bring the car back, I'll ask Stevie-J if I can borrow his phone to call Mr. Wu. Skipping the hair dryer, I wrap a towel tightly around which will spring up the curls. Then, clean white shorts and a clean white T. Flip flops. Pulling off the towel, I scrunch my curls. Life feels simple again.

CHAPTER 21

Up close in bright sun his house takes my breath away. "Oh, my."

What would it be like to live in a huge house like this one? Custom built after his sudden fame and fortune. The gardens are perfect and the grass has sprinklers going full steam keeping it emerald green. Without constant water that grass would be straw then down to dirt in a week. Most of the homes in this town sit on dirt. While I sit in the Corvette pondering this luxury. Do servants clean his house and cook his food? Until a few days ago, Stevie-J and his life were totally separate from mine. Now I'm driving around in his car.

A man carrying a pail and rake comes through an arch cut in a high hedge. I get out of the car waving to him. "Hi! Is Stevie-J at home?"

"Yes, Ma'am, he surely is."

Then I'm undecided what to do. Where to leave the car. Or anything. The man calls out, "Bring it all the way up the drive."

Sensible.

When I park and get out he's disappeared. I walk the

stone path to the front door. It's like the door to a castle with huge black iron hinges and black bolts screwed in the dark wood. Strangely different from the rest of the house which is more modern styling. There's a huge knocker. I knock it. From inside a loud song comes on, maybe Johnny Cash. I don't know if it's on account of my knock or that Stevie-J's sound system just happened to kick in. Or something.

The big door opens. Stevie-J is bare but for his swim suit. Muscles bulging. "I just finished my laps," he says.

"How's the car?"

"Good. Very good."

He slicks back his dark wet hair. "You didn't crash it?"

"'Course not!"

"Just pullin' your chain, Janelle. Just pullin'. You had yer breakfast?" He moves aside for me to step in.

When I do, I'm left breathless. The outside is a confusing mix of very modern with ancient touches. Like that door. Plus a turret sticking up from the roof. Also a lot of glass. The huge windows pull the outdoors in.

"Did you design this house, Stevie-J?"

"Partly. A famous architect from Dallas guided me through the process." I can see he's proud as punch about his house. I notice the furniture is also a strange mix: Tales of King Arthur and Star Trek combined.

"It's beautiful," I tell him. "The whole place is so beautiful." This pleases him no end. He takes my hand and swings it.

"So, anyway, I returned your car and was wondering if I could use your phone?"

"Janelle, we got to get you equipped. You can't live with no communication. What if wolves come in the night? You out there all by yer lonesome in that deserted swamp." He tsk tsks as he picks up a silver phone that looks antique.

Wolves. I never considered that. "Soon as I get some back bills paid I'll get myself hooked up. Meantime, is it OK for me to call Mr. Wu?"

"Mr. Wu Wu?"

I laugh but don't think it's really polite for him to make fun of Mr. Wu. "Yeah, he wants to set me up in some kind of job. Remember the business card?"

Stevie-J folds his arms. "And doin' what exactly?"

"I'm about to find out."

Mr. Wu sounds glad to hear from me. Jumbling my name, he adds, "Very happy you called."

He wants to meet up at The Bluebell. But I'm thinking: *Not that place again. Too many people I know will have their ears cocked our direction: What's Janelle doing with the Chinese wig guy?* I don't need the speculation. I've got the Mel speculation, then the Stevie-J, and now Mr. Wu? Then Darlene coming over with those same sticky menus. No. I don't think so.

"Mr. Wu, if it's all the same to you, why don't we meet at The Public Library on Montgomery Street? It's real quiet in there and we can talk without people interrupting to say hello, you know, that sorta thing."

"Sure! Sure!" he says. "What time is good time?"

"How about noon?"

"Sure! Noon is very good time."

"Ok, great. See you there at noon, Mr. Wu. Bye for now."

I hand the phone back to Stevie-J. He pulls an arm cover off a chair and wipes down the phone.

"Do you think I left germs on your phone?"

He starts laughing like crazy. "I'm cleanin' away the evidence."

Evidence of what?

"C'mon, I'll show you around the place. I'm sorry about all the bruises, Janelle. I'll make it up to you."

I can only imagine. "That's OK," I tell him. "I'll heal."

Grabbing my hand again he pulls me through the enormous living room into an equally enormous dining room. The table is big and long like a banquet from Knights of the Roundtable. "I guess you do a lot of entertaining with your famous friends," I say.

"Not really."

Then we pass through a few more rooms, also large but not huge like the first two. One is a gym with all the machines. Another has official red movie chairs and a movie house screen. Finally we reach the kitchen at the rear. Through giant sliders I can see that famous huge turquoise swimming pool. The one people talk about. It meanders. They say it's like a stream with little bridges and an island.

Off to the side, a naked blonde in a lounge chair is sunning herself. What the fuck?

"I didn't realize you have company."

"Maybelle isn't company. She just comes by to use the pool and keep her tan even."

I'm thinking it's definitely even.

"C'mon, I'll introduce you. You two could be great friends."

"Um… I don't think so. If it's all the same to you."

"What? 'Cause she's got no clothes on?"

You're close, I'm thinking. A rubber Donald Duck bobs in the water. Is that Maybelle's favorite play thing?

He's staring at me, waiting.

"No clothes is a pretty good reason," I say finally.

"Maybelle works in adult entertainment. Her professional name is Margot. It won't phase her. C'mon. Don't be standoffish. She's got a little girl body. Flat chest, and everything but her head is hair free."

Oh, well in that case… "Stevie-J, if it's all the same I prefer not to."

Besides I'm trying to figure out my timing for Mr. Wu. If I'd known my morning would be spent with a naked adult entertainer, I'd have made the Wu appointment even earlier. "Stevie-J, I don't fit into your world."

He passes me an open box of donuts.

"No thanks."

"You wanna take the Vet?"

"You mean to see Mr. Wu?"

He's eating a powder donut straight from the box. It leaves an imprint under his nose. "A hairless woman except for the head?" I say.

"It plays into the school girl fantasy."

"Gee, thanks for explaining. I'm glad it's all on the up and up."

"Janelle, do ya think I'd mess around with *my brand*? Kids are the cement of my brand. It's kids, and teens, who buy all the T-shirts of me holdin' the croc. I'm their idol."

"OK the car would be great. Thanks, Stevie-J."

"Any time," he says, going in for a second donut. "You can hang in the house if that makes you feel happier. I'm goin' back outside. It's rude to leave Maybelle all by her lonesome."

Huh! I'd have thought Maybelle would enjoy some solitude after all her adult entertaining.

"I'll just sit on one of your lovely couches and relax."

"In case you change your mind I'll leave the donuts." He puts the box on the center island then winks. "They're real crispy," he says.

CHAPTER 22

When I walk up the library steps I'm surprised to see Mr. Wu standing under the wide white portico. In this heat I'd have expected him to be waiting inside the lobby. I call out waving. "Mr. Wu!"

"Janelle!" he shouts back with enthusiasm, clutching his hair bag. That bag is like his third arm. Don't think I've ever seen him without it. Of course, I've only seen him when he came to Mel's and that was on hair collection days…

He follows me inside. "Let's go to the room all the way in back," I say. "It's usually empty." I can't imagine what he has in store. I'm pumped and leery at the same time.

His eyes light up when we enter the room. "Very nice room," he says.

Empty but for two other people. "See, it's nice in here." I point saying, "Let's take those chairs by the coffee table." I figure it's a place he can put down his bag. He waits for me to sit then takes the other armchair. The bag stays put on his lap like it's holding diamonds.

"You can put your bag on the table, Mr. Wu."

"Is OK here." He pats it gently like a cherished pet. I'm thinking maybe Mr. Wu carries around a Chihuahua. But that's ridiculous. No air holes showing in the bag.

"I get straight to the point," he says. "You very beautiful, Janelle. Your face can take any hair color."

Is he suggesting I dye my hair? For what reason? As I'm starting to get all hyped up inside, about to tell him *stop right there*, he says, "I want you to be hair model for wigs."

What wigs? Far as I know, Mr. Wu collects the hair and sends it off somewhere to where they make the wigs.

"Um… Mr. Wu, could you be a little more specific?"

"You and me, we travel around, sell wigs."

I knew I was being haunted. I felt it the other night when I sensed a presence. I close my eyes a moment and when I open them, he's still here, the bag still on his lap.

The sun, heating up, is slanting through windows that were in full shade a few minutes earlier. I can feel myself heating up. Little shock waves running heat through my body. Everyone has an idea for my life that will fit *their* purpose.

I stand up stretching and yawning. "I don't see it happening."

Mr. Wu stands almost immediately. He thumps his bag on the coffee table. Unzipping it. Pulling out a cascade of straight, dark auburn hair. "This one look very beautiful on you." He holds out the wig. "Try on. Please."

"In here?" It does seem to be high quality. Not that I've got much wig experience. None, actually. This one is shiny and looks like real hair. I stroke it. Maybe some of Mel's clippings went into this wig. Now I'm finding it less attractive.

"Try on." Mr. Wu shakes it, becoming more assertive.

I sigh, thinking let's get this over and done with. It's a struggle squeezing it over my own long dense curls. Without a mirror I can't tell how it looks. I feel some of my hair sticking out the sides, near my ears, though I try and shove it under the wig.

Mr. Wu yanks it off my head.

"Mr. Wu!"

"You must do correct way." He tucks the wig under one arm and before I can object he ties my hair into a tight knot on top of my head. "Now you put on wig."

Giving him a blistering stare, I slip the wig on. It fits better now. He stands in front of me adjusting it. Then he breaks into a wide smile. I never saw him smile, come to think of it. I doubt Mr. Wu has ever visited a dentist. I have a teeth thing; it's one of my areas. I don't think he ever brushes.

He's beaming. "Beautiful. Go to bathroom, look in mirror."

I feel like telling him to do the same about his teeth. Though I am curious. Dark auburn is a big switch from my bright red. "I'll be right back," I say.

One of the library techies points me toward the Ladies Room. I locate the door in a corner behind stacks of science books. It's locked. Maybe it's a one-zie. I knock but no answer. So now I have to find that techie again and ask for the key. He could have offered me a key to begin with. God almighty. You can almost lose your mind anticipating everyone's every other move. I spot him near the computer station.

"The bathroom key, please." I hold out my hand.

"There ain't no key. You push hard on the door?"

"No! Because you didn't tell me to push!"

He drops his head to the keyboard like I'm not even here.

Going back there I give the door a really hard push. It still doesn't open. I yank off the wig thinking *to hell with all this*, when out pops a woman and her little boy.

I lean against the wall clutching the wig. "Is that a wild animal?" the little boy asks his mother.

CHAPTER 23

Mr. Wu is sitting patiently waiting when I come back holding the wig. Red hair sticking out of the knot. I say, "The Ladies Room is out of order."

"What kind out of order?"

"I don't know. The toilet is clogged or something."

"What kind of place is this?"

"A public place, Mr. Wu. By the way, this is a superior wig."

"Of course! Of course superior!"

He grabs the wig and kind of stuffs it onto my head. "Go to window, see in reflection."

Humoring him, I walk to the window and see my face reflected back; it's cloudy now on this side of the building. But it's not a mirror. But I can make out my reflection pretty well. The wig looks natural. I swing my head and the hair moves across my shoulders with ease. Uneven bangs are a good length.

"So pretty!" He claps, delighted with it all.

"Yeah, it's really nice."

"So you and I business partners in wigs?"

"Wait a sec, Mr. Wu. Business partners how?" I really could use a tall cold Pepsi.

He's rifling through his bag pulling out several sheets of computer size paper. "Contract. You read, Janelle. Then you sign."

I'm experiencing a total out of body moment. Sign? Sign my life away? My first born? Why the hell did I think of that? Raelyn creeping into my subconscious?

I hand him back the wig. "Mr. Wu, I'm not in a good way at the moment. I don't know what turns and twists my life is gonna take." Or is it twists and turns?

"What turns and twists?"

"Ignore me, Mr. Wu, I was thinking out loud. You see, I can't just sign on without knowing every teensy tiny detail about the contract."

He's shaking the papers. "All here, all details. You will be happy."

I don't know what I expected. I suppose coming here led him on. "OK. I'll take these papers home and read them. How's that sound?"

He looks dejected. "Forty-eight hours," he says consulting his black rubber watch.

"What happens after that?"

"Deal is off."

CHAPTER 24

Outside under the front portico we say goodbye politely and go our separate ways. Does he have a car? Come to think of it, I've never seen Mr. Wu's wheels. I only saw him walk into Mel's shop and walk out.

Stevie-J's car is parked over at Label's Garage on the next street. A few people say *Good morning, Janelle* and I respond back. All fakery.

At the garage George Label is acting like pride of ownership, being all silly over the Corvette. He wasn't happy that I wouldn't leave the keys with him. I know how he operates. While I'm gone he goes on a little joy ride with his girlfriend.

"I almost had to move the car," he tells me in a grunt way, putting air in another car's tires.

I grin. "Almost doesn't count."

"Dang you, girl, you could charm the scales off a snake."

Is this another offer of a partnership? Does ole George here wanna make me over into his snake handler? I've heard he keeps a few in a tank. Hanging over his cash register is a picture of that famous model, her long blonde hair, naked body snaking around a giant Anaconda. Or vice versa. I get the shivers just looking at it. "I hate snakes," I say.

"Ain't fond of 'em myself," says George.

Big liar! All the men down here lie, they've honed it to a fine skill.

"Anything else I can do for you today?" he says.

Yeah. I want to have the most spectacular life.

"Bye, bye, George," I say sliding into the Corvette.

When the sparkling Corvette glides down the street people make a point of looking. But I just focus on my driving. God forbid I get in a fender bender, or worse, simply because I dropped my attention from the road.

At Stevie-J's I park in the same spot where I got it. Hoping his little playmate has called it a day. When I hit the big door knocker the music blares out a different tune. It must be programmed. A lady wearing a dark maid uniform opens the door. "He's out back," she says stepping aside. None too friendly, either.

"I'm Janelle."

"Esmerelda." She takes her time looking me up and down so's I'll be sure and know she's boss of the place.

"Nice meeting you." Wow. The woman is an iceberg.

"You mean that?" she says.

"Not quite."

That cracks her up. "You're OK," she says. "Grab yerself a beer from the fridge."

I follow behind her to the kitchen. "Do your friends call you Esme?"

"No they don't. But I don't mind if you do."

Suddenly I want to give her a hug so bad. But I don't want to seem weird, or wear out my short welcome. It's been ages since I hugged anyone strictly out of friendship. Sometimes I think about hugging Mama and Raelyn. That was another lifetime.

"I bet that red hair is all natural," says Esme.

"Inherited from my mom. She's passed on now."

"She gave you a gift. Bless that hair. The curls natural or permed?"

"What are we blessin'?" Stevie-J, come in to the kitchen, is wrapped at the waist in a big striped towel. Droplets cling to his face and hair.

Esme chuckles. "Got to finish up with my vacuuming."

"Everything work out?" he says to me.

"If you mean Mr. Wu, well… it was sort of a surprise."

"Wu? What could be surprising about him?"

"I'd rather skip it for now."

Stevie-J takes two icy beers from the fridge. I roll the bottle across my forehead.

"Wu try and jump your bones?" he says.

"You have a one track mind."

"Relax and take a load off, Janelle." He pats a swivel stool at the pinkish marble center island. It's really long. A mile in countertop life. He sits down patting the stool again. "Will ya take a load off!"

I settle on the stool on his other side, farther away from the glass doors. I'm not in the mood for maybe another of his naked marvels. "Mr. Wu was a total gent."

He swivels the stool to the left. "You sure about that?"

"Yeah I'm sure! Why does everyone give me the third degree? I would know if a man isn't a total gent. I would know in a heartbeat. Why is that so hard for everyone to grasp?"

Esme would grasp it. But she left the kitchen.

Stevie-J slings one arm around my back. "I'm graspin' baby."

I'm hoping Esme will reappear. She's made herself invisible. By orders of Stevie-J is my guess—and that he pays her plenty and off the books.

"Janelle, what you're like is a guitar strung too tight. Everyone knows that sooner or later that string's gonna snap."

"Is the hairless girl still out there?"

"Nope. She did her thirty minutes then went about her way." He's squinting. "Why is it important?"

"No reason." I sip the beer. "This is good, the exact right temperature."

"Of course. I'm no screw up. I have everything nailed down, wired. To perfection. I'm a natural born perfectionist."

Why do those words suddenly make me horny?

He looks at me with a low lidded stare. I look back. "C'mon lil' girl."

With no fuss whatsoever, he scoops me up and carries me to a room that has the biggest bed I've ever seen in my life. The drapes are drawn and the room is dim. When he sets me down I look up into a ceiling of mirror. After that, I only remember how everything felt. All three times.

CHAPTER 25

Stevie-J wakes me with a tall glass of orange juice. And, bottle of gin. "It's tomorrow," he says swinging the bottle by the neck.

"You mean I slept through the whole day into the night and now it's the next day?"

"Yep."

I push up on my elbow. "Wow. I never sleep that long."

"'Course not. You been sleepin' in hell over there." He pours in some gin and hands me the glass.

I have been sleeping in hell. The heat and mosquitoes and the occasional alligator seen strolling around the swamp. The tall glass is frosted. "How'd you get this glass so frosty?" I sip and take another sip. "I don't generally have gin in the morning."

"New life, new patterns." He plops down next to me on the bed.

What does he mean by *new life*? Did he say the same thing to Raelyn? Instead of the gin relaxing me I'm starting to feel jittery. Sure, Raelyn is his long ago past. I doubt she ever gives him a thought. But it feels sort of crummy. Like stealing something from somebody you know really well. Then I remember my forty-eight-hour deadline. Wu. I place the drink on the night table.

"I have to give Mr. Wu my answer soon and I haven't even gone over the contract."

"Screw Wu," he says.

"I owe him the courtesy."

Reluctantly he moves over taking his phone from his pocket. "Here. Use this. Tell him goodbye and goodbye."

Stevie-J is giving me an order? An ultimatum? I really don't care for either. "May I speak in private, please?"

He shrugs. "When you're done, Esmerelda will cook you some breakfast. I already had mine. I been up since six."

"Doing what?"

"Some business." He makes it sound very secretive. Unusual. Normally Stevie-J lets it all hang out. I'm definitely on the watch now.

"You can shower in here," he says, pointing toward a closed door.

Then he leaves the bedroom and I fish around the floor for my shorts where I stashed Mr. Wu's card.

"Wu," he answers.

"Hi Mr. Wu."

"Janelle, very good to hear from you."

"Yes. Well. The thing is, Mr. Wu, I'm not quite decided yet."

"Not decided?"

"No. Not quite."

"OK. I come to your house, speak to you."

"Well, you see, Mr. Wu, I'm not home at the moment. There was a problem and I had to spend the night at Stevie-J's house."

"That the big house with the big castle door?"

"Yes, that's the one."

"OK. We talk there."

I feel somewhat relieved. I don't have to meet him anywhere, and he's already familiar with this house so I won't have to give directions. "So can you come by in an hour, Mr. Wu?"

"Sure."

"OK, great." Though it's anything but great. It's just passable. Like the rest of my life. I lay the phone on the night table. The gin and orange juice seem unappealing now. Or, maybe it's other things. Too damned many to consider.

I hit the shower. Slat steel shelves with all the products imaginable inside a glass shower room big enough for a small party. Luxury. The water pressure is dreamy. It pelts me. I could live in here. Plenty of hot water, too, which is a novelty. The chicken house shower is usually almost all cold from the old water heater. That, alone, come cooler weather, could be my breaking point.

But because of Mr. Wu I have to move things along.

Huge fluffy towels are stacked and hung. A hairdryer hooked on the wall. Too bad I have to hurry. Gobble down some breakfast and saddle up for Mr. Wu. Too bad my clothes are from yesterday. I kind of wanted everything revived and fresh the way I'm feeling right now.

CHAPTER 26

Esme is standing at the 6 burner stove holding a spatula when I enter. She turns around with a knowing gleam in her eye. If I had on a sunshield I could pull it lower. I feel like teenager being called out for bad behavior.

"Good morning," I say.

"Help yourself to coffee, hon. What can I rustle you up for?"

"Oh, it's one of those press coffees. I've never had this at home. I mean in someone's home. Only at the little café on Bell Street. They have a French press and real croissants since they hired the Haitian man."

"No croissants here," she says.

"I didn't mean…"

"How about an omelet to your liking?"

I sit on a swivel stool at the big center island holding my coffee in a white mug. The comfort here is undeniable. I feel like a princess. "Do you have any cheese?"

"What type of cheese do you like?"

"Cheddar?"

"White or the yellow?"

Wow. Two cheddar choices. "Um… I think the yellow, please."

Esme agrees on the yellow, begins cracking eggs, putting my omelet together. Sipping coffee I'm watching, entranced. "Did Stevie-J go on an errand?"

She snorts. "Yeah, to the pool."

Through the sliders I can see the naked girl stretched out on the same lounge chair. Stevie-J on the chair next to her. At least they're not swapping spit. That would make me run from here so fast. I didn't necessarily swallow his story that she comes here strictly to tan. In fact I've kind of lost my appetite. But Esme is already sliding this perfect puffy omelet onto a white plate, then in front of me. "Here you go."

"Oh, thank you, it looks beautiful."

"You want toast, sweet pea?"

"Um… I think just the omelet. And, thank you Esmerelda."

"Just doin' my job."

That kind of waters down the princess mentality I was secretly harboring. "Well, I still thank you."

It is the most terrific omelet I've ever eaten. Esme has

it all over the Haitian man when it comes to omelets, being that her's are fluffier and lighter. "How do you get it so light?"

"It's all in the wrist. You need to whisk them exact. Too much they turn rubbery, but not enough they're all water inside."

All water inside. Stevie-J, out there taking his swim then sitting with his floozy sister. All water inside.

To hell with him. I'll finish my breakfast then get Mr. Wu out of the picture. Then I'll ask Stevie-J to drive me home. *Home home.* It may not be much (actually it's less than not much). At least I don't have to worry about who slept where I slept the night before.

The big door knocker goes off—with *California Dreamin'* blasting through the house. I look at the round wall clock. Mr. Wu. Punctual.

"That would be for me," I tell Esme. "It's Mr. Wu the wig salesman. I can get the door."

She puts up a hand. "Stay right where you are. Finish eatin'. I'll bring him to ya." She smiles at me.

If Stevie-J is so damn wealthy he should hire a man to get the door. "What if you're in the middle of a big banquet cook? You have to stop to answer the door?"

"No big banquets in this house." She's wiping her hands on paper towels. "Just a big house. Cobwebs and the ants are my biggest chore." She takes off her apron to get Mr. Wu. I finish my coffee and set the cup and empty plate and silverware in the sink as Esme instructed. She's very particular about her kitchen. Breakfast with Esme was very pleasant. It's been—I don't know how long since I've thought that and meant it.

She comes back with Mr. Wu trailing. "Coffee, Mr. Wu?" she says.

He looks surprised. I don't think Mel, or any of the other barbershop losers, ever offered Mr. Wu a single cup of coffee.

"Take one, Mr. Wu," I say. "It's French press. Delicious."

He nods and says OK.

"Sit down, Mr. Wu," says Esme. "Sit next to Janelle. You want more coffee, hon?"

"No thank you. I'm filled to the brim."

Esme looks pleased, then goes about pressing one for Mr. Wu.

"How are you today, Mr. Wu?" I ask.

"I am OK." He's scrutinizing my face for what my big answer will be. I keep mum while he sips. Stevie-J appears through the sliders in his swimsuit.

"Hey there, Mr. Wu!"

"Hey to you, Stevie-J. This is beautiful house. Very, very beautiful."

"Yeah. I like it. It came from my crocodile money. And then some."

And then some what? It's the first time I've heard Stevie-J talk about his money coming from other than the damn crocodile. I'm intrigued. But no more is mentioned. Stevie-J invites Mr. Wu for a swim.

"No swim trunks," says Mr. Wu.

"I have dozens. I'll get you a pair that still has the store tags attached. C'mon, it will refresh you. This day is heatin' up fast."

Mr. Wu shakes his head. "I can see pool from here. Very beautiful." He stands up walking closer to the sliders.

"That pool's not all he sees," says Esme.

Transfixed, Mr. Wu stands like a statue.

"That's just Maybelle," I say. "She's naked here every day unless it's raining. Ain't that so, Stevie-J?"

Stevie-J starts cracking up. "It is pretty much the situation."

Mr. Wu opens the sliders and steps out. In silence we watch him walking toward her.

"I best get out there," says Stevie-J. "Janelle you come with me."

"Do I have to?"

"Yeah I think it would be a good idea."

Reluctantly I follow Stevie-J outside.

Maybelle has sat more upright on the lounger. She and Mr. Wu staring each other down.

"The bald pussy talking to me. Giving secret message," says Mr. Wu.

Maybelle screeches. "Get this freak out of here!" Grabbing the towel from Stevie-J's chair, covering herself.

Well, it took Mr. Wu to finally get the job done. Finally she's covered her ass. I squeeze my lips tight to keep from laughing. I want to say *Hats off to you, Mr. Wu.* But he wouldn't get the joke.

Mr. Wu looks undaunted. "Very pretty pussy," he says.

"Listen, Wu." Towering over him, Stevie-J is looking

murderous. It's a side to him that's new to me. It must be the side that gave him the courage to wrestle the croc. Come to think of it, I've never seen this side of Mr. Wu either. Both scary-crazy in their own way. The whole scene is scary crazy. What might happen next?

"OK, that's it, Wu, party over. Ya'll come back inside the house. Maybelle, you stay put. Leave the towel on."

I sort of kind of hate to leave. Curious to see what Mr. Wu has next up his sleeve. He's wearing a short sleeve shirt. For the first time I notice a pile of dark hair on his arms. Plastered down. Like he put on a pomade to keep it smooth. I don't think this much body hair is a common physical trait with Chinese men. At least in the Kung Fu movies. They all seem to be free of body hair. Then he encounters Maybelle without hair and sort of flips out.

"I come back," he shouts to her.

She pulls the big towel up over her head. "*Shut uuuuuuuuup!*"

In the kitchen Stevie-J is all agitated. He doesn't like big noisy trouble. "Wu, you need to leave," he says.

"We haven't talked yet," I say.

"I don't want Janelle," Mr. Wu says. "I want her." He points outside.

My mouth drops open. "For what?"

"Is in the paperwork," he says.

He doesn't want me. Yet he thinks I should find out why by reading a contract he's now going to present to Maybelle?

"What the fuck paperwork?" says Stevie-J. He grabs the hair bag and yanks out some papers.

"Is that different from what you gave me?" I ask Mr. Wu.

"Same."

"This is too much for my brain," says Esme. "I think I'll water the plants and the big fern."

"Mr. Wu, you've disappointed me," I say. I don't even want his damn job but it's the whole idea of it.

He looks ashamed.

Stevie-J whispers, "Shush, Janelle, you'll make him lose face."

I cannot believe I'm being told to shush. Mr. Wu wants to own Maybelle's crotch… yet I'm told to shush.

I'm already exhausted and the day has hardly begun.

That afternoon Stevie-J wakes me from a nap—after the Mr. Wu incident, I went upstairs and sort of collapsed. He lies down next to me all snuggly. We make it again in the big bed. "You're killin' me," he says. I don't tell him that he's a great lover.

CHAPTER 27

He's watching baseball from the bed. His widescreen could be in a movie house. From time to time he lets out a hoot or a boo. I suddenly need to go home. Not that I consider the chicken house my home, it's just a thing my mind does. Other minds too, I guess. I guess if you put your stuff down in an alley, then collect cans all day, at night you go back to that alley to sleep 'cause it's your home. Hoping your stuff is still there where you left it. Plus, I need to pick up clothes and other things. I'm living on borrowed time. Or is it borrowed things? Is there a difference?

"Can you drive me home?"

"You mean now?"

"If you wouldn't mind."

"I thought you liked it here."

"I do. I do like it here. A lot. But I have to go home now."

"Are you worried about Wu? 'Cause if you are, don't be. That nut ain't gettin' back in this house."

"No, no, it's got nothing to do with him. I have to check my bills, do a laundry, that sorta thing."

I'm distancing. I have to. He's so sexy he puts my own sex drive into over-drive. He makes the bottoms of my feet tingle when I get up afterward to pee. I feel a warm spread across my chest which I suspect is actually my heart absorbing all this heat we're stirrin' up.

"Let me just finish out this inning then I'll drive you."

"I appreciate that."

Three hours later he takes me back to the chicken house. Because it's dark now, and the chicken house has no outside lighting, we take the truck 'cause the lights are higher and brighter. He pulls onto the property and aims the truck at where he thinks the door is located.

"No, a little bit more to the right," I say. It is a chicken house no matter how you slice it. And now obviously more so after my few days of total extreme luxury living. "You got it," I tell Stevie-J. The truck lights illuminate the whole shabby mess of it.

He sits staring ahead. "You want me to come in, make sure nobody's hidin' behind the couch?"

"Very funny." As I'm opening the truck door he

reaches for my arm. "Didn't you forget somethin'?"

He kisses me. Gripping my cheeks, long and hard, then puts his hand on my breast and moves it in a circular motion, knowing it will drive me berserk. "I have to go in," I say, gasping.

"OK." He lets go. "A girl's gotta do what a girl's gotta do."

"You're a good guy, Stevie-J, thanks for being so understanding."

Of what? It's not like we got married over the past few days. Or that we're even engaged or anything. I think I'm a bit carried away—what with the great home cooked meals, wide screens in every room, all the rest of it. And, the bathrooms. I'm just in love with those big clean bathrooms. I shudder thinking of my shower stall.

"Bye for now," I say, stepping down from the truck.

The ground is soft underfoot. He's keeping the truck lights on. I have this sensation of alligators slinking around the trees. When a web of Spanish Oak brushes my face I jump. Fearful. For no particular reason. I've come back here on my bike in the dark at least a zillion times.

I get the door open. He toots twice. I step inside, smell the dank. The fairy tale has ended. This is real life. Too real.

It's the same shit hole. No angels with handy-man skills gave it a makeover like this show I watched at Stevie-J's. That crew smashing out the walls and putting up new drywall and rolling on fresh glossy paint. New flooring of that wood that isn't real wood. Not that you could ever tell. Nope. No angels here, no such luck. You have to be holy to interest the angels. I've been fucking. Drinking. Eating too much rich food. Fucking my sister's ex-boyfriend, no less. The man she had a baby with, and might have even married if the baby had lived. Who knows what Raelyn might have done.

What little there is in here is exactly like before. I touch a loose string from a missing button on the Barcalounger and a sob bursts out. Then something occurs to me. Before I left there were four missing buttons. I'm counting five missing now. Five loose strings dangling from the Barca. Down on the floor, all by itself, is the fifth button. How could that happen?

I walk through the flow. Everything else seems unchanged. Maybe the angels did come down wanting to help, took a look around, flew over to Stevie-J's, and saw me engaged in what are considered unnatural acts in this state. Of course the angels flew away.

The nice life at Stevie-J's dissolves in an instant. I heard through the grapevine that a guy who once lived here committed suicide. There's some disagreement over whether it was before the place was semi-fixed up, or while it still had all the chicken coops and other chicken paraphernalia.

I'm thinking I should get on my bike and ride to the phone booth that's still hooked up in Haber's Ice Cream Parlour. Explain to Stevie-J that I made a huge mistake and could he come back and pick me up?

"No! No! No!" I scream out, calling myself some pretty foul words. It's the worst possible idea. I go in the bathroom and sit on the bowl. When I get up to wash my hands, scrawled across the mirror in deep pink, what could only be lipstick, is the word *HELP*.

"Oh god almighty!" This comes out of me as a long screeching wail. I scream again, almost hysterical, like my head is about to explode. I knew the place felt haunted. Someone, or some thing, has been in here. Too creepy—what kind of *HELP* did they mean?

Rushing outside I scrabble around in the dark for my bike. I have to pedal slow in the soft mush. When I reach County Road 213 I start pedaling my brains out. Soon I'll reach Haber's. In under 5 minutes at this speed.

When I ride up the place is jammed with people coming and going, the usual crush around the entrance where they sell the homemade chocolates. I leave my bike in the dark side alley and bolt for the door, kind of pushing through the crowd, most who know me.

The old phone booth is empty. People use their cell phones. I pull the wooden door inward to shut out the racket. Stevie-J picks right up. Habers showing on his phone must've had him wondering. "Stevie-J, it's me, Janelle, pick me up, it's crucial!"

"What's going on?"

I'm so upset out of breath I can barely get the words out. "Someone was in the chicken house while I was gone. They wrote help in lipstick on the bathroom mirror."

I can hear him chuckling. "No offense, Janelle, but I'd be writin' a hell of a lot of *helps* if I was stuck in that place."

"I don't think it's a joke or a prank. I'm scared to be there. Please take this serious, Stevie-J."

"It's probably some chicken ghost come back to haunt you."

The booth is starting to feel claustrophobic. Maybe Raelyn got this casual kind of reaction from Stevie-J when she informed him of her pregnancy. I always wondered how he would act in a true crisis.

I give it one last try. "I think you should pick me up from Haber's and come see the writing for yourself."

There's silence.

"Are you still there?"

"Still here. OK, I'll be there in a few minutes."

"I stashed the bike in the alley. Meet me where the alley dips down, so the crowd outside won't see us."

"Ten four."

I can't stand *that ten-four*. It means Stevie-J still has doubts. Does he think I'm crazy? Someone with too-pink lipstick wrote Help. In the place where I live. I don't have pink lipstick. It has to be a woman who carries it in her purse. It could be anyone. It could be me.

CHAPTER 28

I'm watching for him in the shadows between buildings. The sky is dark with few stars. The silver truck comes gliding along the other side of the road, which is actually a good idea. Stevie-J can pass by Haber's from the other side then make a U up near the Greek Restaurant, then drive to the alley dip where I'm waiting. No one will be the wiser.

Without a word he gets out of the truck and chucks the bike in back. I get this sort of man in charge flexing his muscles feeling coming off him. Then he makes another U and drives away from all the Haber's fuss.

"You have to see for yourself," I tell him. "Just the way *HELP* was scrawled—desperation! Desperation in that pink slippery lipstick. I'll take this to my grave."

"If you say so."

What? I look over at him. Bland. Where is the muscled man who just chucked my bike in this truck and excited my boob less than an hour ago? Has he disappeared, and this new man, this clone, taken up residence? What's going on here? I've seen too much that can't be explained. Not just seen, but heard, smelled, felt things brush my arms, for instance; or my head. I blamed it all on Mama who was always too needy for her own good. I figured she wanted to reach me past the grave.

"I'll leave the lights on and the truck runnin'," he says.

"Did I happen to interrupt your life tonight, Stevie-J?"

"Nope. Was watchin' the game."

The fucking game. I don't even ask which one. "Come in, please."

He follows me in. Then on into the bathroom. "That there is one small shower," he says.

"I'm aware."

"Look." We both stand there staring at *HELP*.

Stevie-J starts laughing. "'Course it looks desperate. It's meltin' in this hot pot."

"Someone came in and wrote on the mirror. They didn't write hello, or fuck you. They wrote *HELP*."

He's scratching his back under his T-shirt. "I don't know, Janelle, I think it's a hoax. Somebody sees yer place dark a few nights, jiggles in with a credit card and screws with yer head."

I take a breath. He just might have a point. Due to the sketchy wiring I never leave a lamp on. I'm feeling a little less afraid now and a slight bit ridiculous. But still not convinced. "I'm not convinced."

"In that case you're gonna have to call in The Feds. And they're so busy battling the anti-this-ers, the anti-that-ers, I don't think The Feds are gonna give ya the time a day. I say we should clean it off."

He probably has a point. "Should I wash it off the mirror or Windex?"

"Sweets, it's up to you."

"That shade of lipstick, so bright pink and outdated—does it look familiar?"

He folds his arms and leans closer. "Hmmm…"

"See! I knew there was something fishy. Nobody would be caught dead in that color. Nobody I know. It must be someone passin' through that both of us saw then forgot about."

"So why would she end up at your place markin' her spot like a dog at a hydrant?"

"I don't know."

"You wanna come back with me?"

His nice big bed with the cool percale sheets. The

cappuccino machine makes such a thick froth.

"It's a hot box in here." His face is sweating. "I think it was a guy did it."

"Huh?"

"HELP. From a man."

"No way. That's a woman tactic."

"I'll leave the bike up against the house."

He didn't say coop. Or chicken. He said house.

"Do you think this place could somehow be remodeled?"

He's wiping his face with a tissue.

"This place?" He shakes his head. "No."

CHAPTER 29

Come morning, I still haven't cleaned *HELP* off the mirror. It mesmerizes me. A few wipes of wet paper towel it would be gone lickety split… Yet, somehow… removing this silent cry, or call for mercy, or whatever the fuck… kind of seems to be a sacrilegious act. *You'll never get to heaven if you break my heart, so be very careful not to…*

Could it be Raelyn in trouble? And possibly counting on me? Slim chance. Raelyn, like Mama, suffers a slight claustrophobia. Wearing a mask all the way from Spain I'd have to commit her.

Running the shower in the tiny bathroom steams it up and melts *HELP* into a pink slosh down the glass.

Throwing on red shorts and a black T, black flip-flops with rhinestones, a twist of my hair into a pony—well my life may be a total wreck but at least I put my best foot forward.

Breakfast. I need some. Except the milk carton feels tepid. All that food I bought—finito. The fridge has gone on the fritz. What else???

I can't continue living this way. If only Esme were my Esme. My only choice for breakfast is The Bluebell again.

CHAPTER 30

The front bike tire is looking soft. More what else. Wobbly, it gets me to The Bluebell. *One day at a time*, as the saying goes. Except I'm not abusing anything. Except, possibly, myself. Do they have groups for that sort of thing? You probably have to be a cutter or anorexic or bulimic to fit those groups. I'm none of that. Yet for me, even *one second at a time* may be too ramped up. What should I do, sit in a chair all day? Naked like Maybelle?

People turn and look when they see me enter. Obviously the word is out on me and Stevie-J. Some deliberately shield their mouths when I pass by, so I can't hear what they're saying. I understand why Sly got out. These small towns can tear you apart.

I take a seat at the counter—fine by me. Stools with comfy padded backs. About two-thirds are occupied. Mostly by men who spread their newspapers on the counter while they wait on the food. That can be annoying, they get in your space. I sit in an empty next to the vet, Dr. Milway, on the chance he may have gotten his jabs by now. He is a vet so he must be used to jabbing cows and whatnot.

"Hi Janelle."

"Hi, Doc."

The conversation stalls there.

My paper placemat lists all the cities worth mentioning in Italy. I wonder if I'll see a one of them in my entire life? It's interesting how Italy is shaped so artistic, while many countries are flat and squared off. It must be Italian Night here. They vary the nights with the foods of different countries. Behind the counter little Italian flags stick up in water glasses on the shelf. Italian Night is extremely popular since most people like spaghetti and meatballs and garlicky bread. Spumoni is served for the dessert. Another favorite is German Night with so many families stretching back to Germany. They usually serve two types of strudel for dessert. As I'm studying the map, I hear loud clapping. Looking up in time to see Stevie-J has come in. His fans acknowledging him. You hold a scary animal over your head you get fans.

A hand rests on my shoulder. I look up into his eyes. "Janelle, order yet?"

I shake my head.

"Let's move to a booth."

The Doc offers to slide one stool down, but Stevie-J tells him not to trouble himself.

We settle in a booth. His face is serious, not his usual jolly-jokey. A young new waitress drops two menus on the table. Stevie-J hands me one then opens his own. "Open your menu Janelle." His voice is low.

I do as he says. "What's going on?"

"Talk lower," he says. "After I dropped you off last night I get this strange call. From Wu."

"Mr. Wu?"

"Yeah."

"What did he want?"

"That's where it gets confusing. I say to him: I suppose you're callin' to inquire about Janelle and the wigs. And he says: No more Janelle, screw Janelle."

"Mr. Wu said that about me?"

"He sure did. And, more."

The waitress comes back and fills both our cups from the silver coffee pot. She's standing a little close to Stevie-J.

"I thought I might have tea," I say to needle her. She arches one eyebrow. "I can change it."

"No, no. That's all right." But my tone is saying it's

not all right. She looks embarrassed. She can have him; but only when I say so.

"You can leave the pot," he tells her. Giving her one of his damn winks. Her subtle enthusiasm isn't lost on me. Stevie-J huddles behind his menu again so I do the same.

"Wu said he found himself the perfect partner for his enterprise."

"He called it an enterprise?"

Stevie-J puts down the menu to take a sip. "Wait it's scalding." Then he says, "Yeah, an enterprise." He's gazing around. Nobody's paying attention to us, they've had their fill and moved on to other gossip.

"What else?"

"That was it. He hung up."

I sit back in the booth. So big deal. Wu has an enterprise. I don't get where Stevie-J is going with this.

"Put up your menu again, Janelle."

Oh, Jesus Christ.

"Remember when he said all that weird stuff to Maybelle, about talkin' to her pussy? All that?"

"Who could forget?" I say.

"That's when it hit me. Who wears that shade of pink lipstick?"

"I never took him to be a cross-dresser."

"Not Wu!!!" People are looking up now, and Stevie-J crouches lower, the two menus pitched like a little tent. "Maybelle. Maybelle wears that color. Remember? It's Maybelle who wrote on yer mirror, Janelle."

He slaps the menu down just as the waitress comes back.

Stevie-J rattles off: "Two eggs sunny-side, crisp bacon, hash browns, toast and jam."

"You?" she says stiffly.

"The same, but no jam, I'll take butter."

"I solved it." He sits back triumphant.

"Just 'cause she wears that shade?"

"I left out the best part."

I stick my elbow on the table and stare out the window at a mess of birds pecking a grass patch. "Bring it on."

"Today's a hot sunny day right? But… there's no Maybelle at my pool."

"What!!!"

"That's what I'm tryin' to tell ya. Wu abducted her. Who knows what for? Maybelle ain't no slouch but if she was screaming *HELP* on your mirror it's worth a call to the cops. So don't linger over yer breakfast. Don't rush but don't linger."

If he was planning on making a cop call, why did we order two enormous breakfasts? And a whole coffee pot? Why not coffee to-go and a sweet roll? If you're in a big hurry, you don't order eggs and the works in here.

"Stevie-J, why didn't you phone the cops as soon as you got this figured out?"

"Janelle. This is your collar. It was your place, your mirror. You figured out it was a woman. You called it *her call for help.* You were her call for help, you Janelle. I'm just an innocent bystander." He sips his coffee. "It's cooled down some," he says.

"My collar? What am I a police woman now? I'm an innocent bystander, too! Can I help it who breaks in while I'm gone? Stevie-J, you are losing it. You are losing it so bad! I know it's that shit with the opium you've been smoking."

"Didn't I tell you that first night at Karaoke I would help you get rich and famous?"

"What of it?" I don't even feel like eating.

"This here what we've got is a major news story. It basically landed in yer lap. Everyone's going after the Asians. They want to blame the covid spread on someone, instead of their own dumb selves for not following the doc's advice," he says.

"You don't know for sure that Mr. Wu took Maybelle."

"Who else? Put two and two together over the last 24 hours and you'll come up with nine. Which makes Wu meat for the grinder. The papers will send reporters and camera men to yer door. You'll open it, all beautiful and sweet, telling them about Wu and his plans for you that didn't work out. Then the sudden disappearance of Maybelle. The lipstick on the glass. Damn! That lipstick *Help* will push the story to international news."

I drop the sugar packet I picked up out of nervousness. I don't dare tell him *HELP* is now a slight pink stream.

"People like two things, Janelle. They like a hero and they like to hate. Keep those in mind. You'll do the Dr. Phil and the morning talk shows. The View. That's a perfect one for a sweet southern gal like yerself. Wait till you see the money come flyin' in in wheel barrow loads."

Stevie-J is beaming. "I made you a promise. Human nature and circumstances and bad luck for Maybelle took care of the rest."

The waitress returns holding a round tray heaped with breakfast.

"Dig in," he says. "Then we'll go public with your story."

"It's not *my story*. I refuse to mention Mr. Wu! Someone might attack him. I can't have his blood on my hands."

"Your story, your choice." He looks disappointed.

"It's not *my story*! Stop calling it that! And what about Maybelle, she could be dead."

"That's the tragedy of it."

CHAPTER 31

He spurs me on to eat faster. I don't even taste my food. I want to say to him: *You're of two minds*. I eat half, he eats everything. Then we get up and leave.

The police station is on Locust. I refuse to get out of the car. He makes a lot of loud arguments and then I start worrying that his version of *his truth* might harm Mr. Wu. "Don't you know that circumstantial evidence is the weakest link in the legal system?" I say. "People have gotten the chair based on circumstantial evidence."

"How do ya know all this legal beagle stuff?"

"I watch Crime Fighters."

"Then you better come in and help me keep the story straight," he says. "Since it's really your story and I'm just helping you get it out."

"It's not my story!!!" I scream so loud a woman walking her dog hears me and looks over.

The cops all know Stevie-J and make a fuss, then the downstairs cops send us up to the upstairs cops. They make a fuss, too, before sending us in to The Captain.

He listens to the story and seems bored. "It's speculative. This Maybelle… what was the last name?"

"Short. Maybelle Short. A local girl, Captain."

"College girl?"

"Not exactly. Though I think at some point she got herself qualified."

"You talkin' about a girl workin' 9 to 5? Or a workin' girl?"

Stevie-J is looking flushed around his neck. I've never seen him flustered. I don't think he quite planned on having an *up close and personal* about Maybelle and her life. If she still has one. The Captain is prodding him. Stevie-J, so far, has not mentioned that Maybelle works in adult entertainment. The Captain hears that, he'll kick us out so fast. Everyone knows that type of work is all about risk. Around here, the cops don't do risk. They put on their blinders and get slobbering drunk and stick twenties in g-strings. When something in this town actually does go wrong, the cops here don't understand what you're talking about. You could be talking in tongues for the amount of time and attention they'll give you.

"Then there's Mr. Wu," says Stevie-J. "He plays a big part. A very big part would be my guess."

"His real name is Wuchinski," I say.

"What the fuck!" Stevie-J lets out. "Who ever heard of a Chinese guy named Wuchinski?"

The Captain motions at me with a limp finger. "What's she here for?"

"Like I said earlier, Captain, it was Janelle who found the lipstick writing on her bathroom mirror."

"Right," says The Captain.

"This young lady is Janelle."

"I know." He smiles fast and fake, clipping papers with a stapler. "OK, then. I'm gonna need to speak with Maybelle. Before we can take this any further."

"The Captain goes to Mel's," I say in a low voice.

Stevie-J passes me a look. "That's the thing. We can't find Maybelle."

"You live with her?'

"No. Ya see, she comes by my pool every day to work on her tan. Today she ain't been seen by anyone on the property. And of course Janelle is the one who got the writin' on..."

The Captain stands up. "OK. I think I got it all. Folks, thanks for comin' in. Nice to see you, Janelle."

I stand up right away but Stevie-J stays put. "So you're gonna go on a hunt for Wu? Wuchinsky? He's a priority, right? 'Cause he is at the center of this puzzle. Dead center, no pun intended."

"You seem to have a good feel fer the case," says The Captain. "Why don't you work it as a P.I.?"

"You jokin' with me?"

The Captain laughs good naturedly. "Get the hell out of my office before I have you both arrested for wastin' taxpayer dollars."

We exchange looks and make tracks. On the street I say, "That went real well."

"I ain't done. By no means is this over."

"Last night you didn't want to even talk about it. What kind of drugs you taking, Stevie-J?"

He puts both arms around me, holding me tight. "Love drugs. I'm on the love mobile." He squeezes my ass in full sight of anyone on the street. I feel his erection poking my stomach. "I need to fuck you so bad, Janelle."

"What about Maybelle gone missing?"

"It's just one day. And what's this Wuchinsky all about? She can take care of herself. You can't. You need me. I'm your guy."

Exactly what I don't need.

CHAPTER 32

ack at his place we hit the bed a while. Then we both walk naked through the house and out to the pool. His idea. It's Esmerelda's day off. The gardener's, too. "I want us always to be natural one with the other," says Stevie-J.

Does he think his yard is the Garden of Eden?

He runs the diving board then canon-balls off rather than taking the dive. First time I've ever seen a naked diver. It's not all that exquisite. I'm sitting at the shallow end with my legs dangling in the water. Already my nipples are burning. "My nipples are getting burnt," I tell him.

"You're a redhead, goes with the territory."

"Yeah, well, my territory is burning up fast. You have any number 50 Coppertone?"

The rim tiles on the pool are really hot; even though I doused them with water before I sat down. "These tiles are gonna burn a pattern in my ass," I tell him.

He paddles over and pulls me in. We hang there a while, the water cool and delicious. "You could have this every day," he says, putting a finger inside me under the water. When I come, my body shuddering, he winds me up again.

"No more," I say, collapsed against him in the water, arms around his neck.

"If you were a bird youda been a Raven."

"What would you have been, Stevie-J?"

I'm straddling him my legs around his waist. He sucks my tit. "I would be a suckling lamb," he says. I ain't in the bird category."

"How do you know?"

"Lamb of God takes away the sins of the world."

"Then fix it, Stevie-J. Once and for all I want someone to goddamn fix things!"

"Don't use God's name in vain."

"How can you go about with all this fucking and sex stuff then lecture me on God?"

"God made me a fucking man. You, Janelle, he made a point of entry. How else we gonna get to where we need to as a civilization?"

"Are you talking about making babies?" Without turning them from alligators into crocodiles.

"Unless you want the entire species to die out. Yeah, it's what I'm talkin' about."

He sounds annoyed. He's been slightly off his game since The Captain basically told us to drop dead. I think that's why we're naked. Like he's thinking: Here's my incredible big swimming pool, Captain, you can kiss your sorry ass before you ever get invited over to take a dip.

I say, "The entire species dead? I don't think so, thanks very much. I guess it's your delivery that is a bit…"

"My delivery? My delivery is what bought this swimmin' pool. And, then some. You want delivery, go on back to Mel and open his mail."

I've never seen him so crazy worked up. "It's Maybelle's got you so upset, am I right?"

"For fuck sake, ya got that part right. Maybelle is my half a sister."

CHAPTER 33

Mr. Wu, or Mr. Wuchinsky, or Mr. Wuchinski, as the news headline might flash across the screen: *IS A PERSON OF INTEREST.* Not by them; by Stevie-J. Obsessed with finding Mr. Wu. Or as he calls him, with blood fangs practically dripping from his mouth: WuWu.

Having analyzed the whole situation, I have come up empty. Maybelle sunbathing naked in front of her brother, even a half-brother, is downright creepy. Call me modest. I no longer want to screw Stevie-J. Incest in these parts is commonplace. Call me paranoid.

We're at an impasse. I refuse to fuck him any further. He's freaking out. I'm also starting to question the status of his virus vaccinations. When I asked to see his little card, he balked. Told me it was his personal business. I told him that it's my business, too, being that we've been so *personal.*

All of it has left me unhinged. If there's one thing I do not want it's that virus in my body. "I'll help you find Margot, but only from a distance," I tell him.

"She's Maybelle," he says, fury clouding his eyes.

"Not in her world. And I bet Mr. Wu calls her Margot." I almost say *especially when he talks to her pussy.*

It's almost like, in an odd way, Mr. Wu (chinski) (chinsky) has become Chillin' Millie. Both of them talking to things that can't quite answer back. Not in the usual way. Though I suppose if Margot and Mr. Wu are intimate, guaranteed her pussy is talking up a storm.

I've taken to sleeping in a separate bedroom in the mansion. Not that there aren't bedrooms to spare. This place being massive. Stevie-J is triple furious with me now. He takes off early in the morning, before I'm up, usually in the Corvette. When I go out front to see the new flowers planted every day, I mostly see the truck parked and the Corvette nowhere. I have a nice chat with the gardener who tells me the flower names. Stevie-J doesn't come back till after dark. When he does.

Breakfast I spend chatting with Esme. A fun breakfast like we're old friends plus she's not grabbing me every other minute. Plus she's such a phenomenal cook.

After breakfast I put on a swim suit, like a normal person (not like Maybelle-Margot) and I swim through the twists and turns of the huge turquoise pool. Ducking to swim underwater when I come to the little low foot bridges built across the narrow parts where the pool is designed to look like a meandering stream. Lovely thick foliage hangs over. It's the most peace I can remember. Stevie-J can stay away the whole year as far as I'm concerned. Anyhow, he'll probably kick me out. I feel no guilt. He smelled my troubles and lassoed me like a young calf right into his life style. Besides, Esme is way more interesting. Born and raised in the far north of Maine, her daddy was a salesman and worked the whole eastern coast. Eventually he moved the family down here.

"Why down here?" I ask her. Maine sounds so much better, with its short summers and snow bending the branches.

"I don't know for sure," she says. "I think my Muzzy couldn't take the cold what with her rheumatism."

Well, that makes sense. Here is a person who can talk sense. I think it's because her young brain developed in another section of the country. Down here they still get all dewy-eyed over the Confederate Army. Take Mel, with his Confederate shampoo capes. And all his old, crusty leftover Confederate customers. So many times I just wanted to scream: Get with the times! If I had, he would have fired me on the spot. I should have screamed out my feelings. 'Cause it turned out I'm gone from there anyway.

"Esme, do you think I should move up north?"

She tilts her head considering this. "It would be a big change. Ya might not like it. But, then again, ya might. What the heck," she says, "what's to lose?"

We both know she means Stevie-J.

She smiles knowingly. Esme looks almost pretty when she smiles. "You'll get a sign when it's the right time. Here, hon," she says, passing the basket of cinnamon buns, "have them while they're still warm."

CHAPTER 34

He barrels in before suppertime. Hardly gives me a glance; like I'm a lamp that's burned out. Until he tells me squarely to leave, I'm staying put. They can torch that old chicken house for all I care. I've had a taste of the good life, and it's pretty damned incredible.

Five or so minutes go by and he re-enters the room where I'm lying on the couch reading an Ellery Queen mystery that's serialized in the local paper. The rest is all ads and junk. I used to read it at Mel's so naturally I'm thrilled it gets delivered here, too, so I can keep up. I only missed a few issues so I can pretty much fill in what went down. The woman with the blonde bouffant hair-do has escaped her rotten husband by going to Mexico with a guy she met in a bar. He's not Mexican but he does business in Juarez. I don't know his exact business which may have been spelled out in the few chapters I missed.

"Comfortable?" he says.

"It beats my old Barcalounger."

He gives me a cold stare.

"Do you want me to go home?"

I can see he's hemming and hawing. "What I want, Janelle, is for you to help me find Maybelle."

The couch is so comfy, it's like floating on a fluffy cloud. "What is this couch stuffed with?"

"Horse shit."

Hmm. "How can I be expected to find Maybelle? I don't know her favorite haunts. I don't know her friends." Or her strip clubs and god knows where else.

He sits at the other end of the long couch. He looks pretty wiped out. What sister could be worth so much effort? I'm thinking of Raelyn. Did he go after her with the same intensity when their baby died then she skipped town? Not hardly. I almost tell him this.

"But you know Wu," he's saying. "You know people who know Wu. You could sniff around and dig up stuff. This whole thing centers around Wu."

The thought of sniffing out Mel and the old barber clients takes the wind of out my sails. Just as I was starting to get it back, what with the long cool sleeps under the fluffy comforter, Esme's incredible meals, and of course the pool. I can see all that is about to change. He's getting ready to toss me. I'm worth nothing, really, to him; and vice versa. It's understandable. Though I still don't get why finding Maybelle is such a big deal. She was living a life of scum. Does Stevie-J think he's going to bring her back to the lord?

"OK."

"You sayin' you'll give me a hand findin' Maybelle?"

"Sure." Just because she's a total slut and loser. And 'cause I don't exactly have a choice in the matter if I want to keep this new lifestyle a while longer. "I'll see what I can find out."

Now he's smiling ear to ear.

"So when do you want me to start becoming Miss Marple?"

"Who?"

"It's a joke. When do you want me to start?"

"Tomorrow. Nobody Wu did business with hangs around at night."

"OK." It is the least I can do. I suppose.

Deliriously happy, he picks up a toss pillow and heaves it at me. "So you'll be movin' back in the big bedroom with me."

I just stare at him until he realizes that is not what I had in mind. I hug the toss pillow to my chest. "Stevie-J, let's take it one step at a time. I agreed to be a P.I. on the Maybelle case, but I'm going to sleep in the other bedroom a while longer."

He's fuming again, gets up pacing the room. "What's one got to do with the other?" He bends unlacing his sneakers, throwing them against a wall.

"You just made extra work for Esme." I get up and check the wall. "Yep. As I suspected. Filthy dark sneaker marks. You got any of that Clorox Clean Up spray?"

"How the hell should I know?"

I could say the same thing back about taking on Maybelle's case. I could say *How the hell should I know* and wash my hands of it. 'Cause what do I know about following leads? Nothing! Yet he wants me in this because he doesn't feature doing it alone. I want to yell *Well how do you think Esme will feel seeing this filth on a formerly clean wall?* The whole thing has left me exhausted.

I lie back down on the couch.

"If you continue to provoke me, Stevie-J, I'm going to have to drop out. Do you get it? I cannot do that kind of close work if I feel exhausted from your tirades."

He drops his head a moment and actually looks sorry.

"Go to the slop room and see if Esme has any Clorox Clean Up. Bring it here, I'll clean the damn marks off the wall, myself," I say.

Standing in his own huge living room he's looking out of sorts.

"This is what I mean, Stevie-J. You don't know which end of the stick, and that just totally bugs me. I mean, so much you have no idea."

He says nothing.

"OK. It's all in your court now. Leave the Clorox near the stains." I close my eyes, wait, then take a peek. He's left the room. Anything and everything between us is now on the table.

CHAPTER 35

Waking slowly, I can't stand the thought of getting up and pounding the pavement to gather clues about Maybelle's disappearance. As far as I'm concerned she can stay lost forever. She and Wu. I suppose he's capable of anything with Maybelle at his side.

Esme is doing homemade waffles in a big waffle iron. I've never seen waffles of such golden beauty. She slides a plate of two in front of me. I gobble them down. "These are so fantastic," I tell her. Pleased, she asks if I want another serving. Her waffles are huge. "Two is my limit," I tell her, patting my stomach. "Thank you, Esme."

"You spending the day in the pool, I presume?"

"Don't I wish. I can only take a quick dip then I have to get myself out there hunting down Maybelle."

She makes a sound like a bull about to scratch dirt. "I knew right off she's no good. All that nakedness ain't normal. She wants everyone to look. Troy, the last gardener quit. Afraid he'd get carried away and cheat on his new wife. Didn't matter to her who—like she was soliciting out there. Once she signed a package from UPS totally naked."

"Gross."

Stevie-J comes rambling in straight to the coffee press. "So, Janelle, I'm gonna let ya take the truck. The Corvette is too high profile, everyone will see ya and word will get out. Wu will go straight into hiding. Just what we don't want. There's a million silver trucks on the road, you'll blend in."

"Oh, goody." Like Wu's not already in some kind of hideout. "I'll take a quick swim and be on my way."

He pours his coffee over ice. "Cheers," he says. I don't sense he is very cheerful at all. "You're mean, Janelle. To cut me off in the bedroom."

After I get myself ready I go in search of Stevie-J for the truck keys. He's on his phone and motions me to wait.

"Take this credit card, too," he says. "The truck uses up a lotta gas."

Where does he expect I'll be travelling to? I take the card and shove it in my sack purse.

"And you'll be needin' meals and lodging," he continues.

"What???" I can feel the hair stand up on the back of my neck. "Where exactly do you expect me to go? Around the world in eighty days?"

"Funny."

"Not funny. I plan on staying within the county line. That's it. Take it or leave it. Next thing you'll be sending me on freighter to Southeast Asia."

"Wu's Asian," he says. "It could be a possibility."

"Wuchinsky is not an Asian name, with either the y or the i. It's made up. Mr. Wu must've been on the lamb all along, taking us all for a ride. Mel included."

"Janelle, I've thought this out long and hard. Wu has skipped to where he feels safe and knows the lay of the land. I think eventually we'll find him in China."

I start laughing hysterically. "*We?*" I can hardly catch my breath. "*We* are not going to China. *We* are staying within county lines. Have you thought about hiring a real P.I.? Someone who will know the ropes? Have you considered that? Well have you!"

"You don't have to yell. My head's poundin'."

"Well, I didn't mean to but this is getting so crazy!"

Esme hasn't been able to get a word in edge-wise. A few times her mouth opened then closed.

"I think Esme would like to speak, Stevie-J."

"What about?"

"I'm putting in my notice," she says.

"For what?"

"She's quitting! She can't stand living in this nut house anymore! Who could blame her? I almost can't stand it myself. But I'm not employed by you. I'm just your friend tryin' to help."

Esme turns and leaves the room.

"She can't just quit like that!" he says.

"Grrrr...."

CHAPTER 36

The first place I hit is Mel's barbershop. He looks kind of shocked, like maybe he's thinking I've come a-begging for my old job back.

"I'm just here for a visit," I tell him.

"Well ain't that convivial."

Nothing much is changed. He continues trimming the beard of some guy draped in one of the Confederate capes.

"How's business?" I say, taking an empty chair.

"Business is business."

No question he can hold a grudge.

"I've been kind of busy myself." I don't say what and he doesn't ask. This is going to be more difficult than I anticipated. "The shop looks good, very tidy."

"Yeah. Mr. Wu has been giving me a hand. Since you left. Out of the blue."

Mr. Wu! I almost jump out of the chair. Gathering my composure, I say, "But isn't Mr. Wu busy with his wig stuff?"

Mel gives me a funny look: *like why this sudden interest in Mr. Wu.* "Yep, he's got the wig thing goin' with an assistant now. More freedom for him to freelance and whatnot."

Just incredible! There's Stevie-J searching high and low and Mr. Wu has been right here under our noses. And, Maybelle—must be the assistant. A laugh that I'm trying to hold back comes out as a gurgle. "Is he coming in today? Mr. Wu? I'd like to say Hi."

"Nope. Tomorrow or the next day. Tilt yer head back a bit," he says to his customer, Randy.

Standing up, I say, "It's been swell seeing ya, Mel. As the saying goes Rotsa Ruck!" He should only know I'll be scouting from across the street watching for Wu's return.

"Hold on there a minute, Janelle. Sit yerself back down. I'm almost done here and I wanna talk to you a minute."

Twice in one sentence he said *minute*. This could drag out. I'm not in the mood for a long chat. This new information has raised my spirits considerably. I might even sleep with Stevie-J tonight. I am a bit horny and that is one man who can get the job done. And, then some. Then I'm thinking it's strange—how Mel didn't mention Maybelle by name.

He finishes up with Randy, takes the guy's money, the usual stupid jokes are exchanged.

"What's up?" I'm just dying to get back in the pool.

Mel sits in a customer chair. "I've heard rumors."

I look back at him unblinking. Any shit about me and Stevie-J I am out of here so fast.

"Janelle, you know a lot of people in this town. We both do. Being that we both been here forever."

Huh! "Don't remind me."

"You ever know a gal named Margot?"

What the fuck! "Can't say I do."

"Well, our Mr. Wu has up and married this Margot. From the way he talks, the sun rises and sets on her."

Wu and Maybelle married. Whoa! Stevie-J is gonna have twenty-five shit fits.

"Have you met her?" I ask Mel.

"Not yet."

I yawn to make out I'm bored. "Well, if that's all you have to say… I've got to be going now. Errands. That sort of thing."

"Will you be passing by here again? After the errands?"

Does he want me to pick up something for him? "No, I'm going over to Shrenksville."

"On your bicycle?"

Mel is taunting me like a dog after a hot dog on a stick. Except I ain't biting.

"If you must know, I borrowed Stevie-J's truck."

"That silver one?"

"It's the only truck he owns."

"Funny."

Now what's he jabbering about? "What is funny about a silver truck?"

"It's just that I seen him in a bright blue one just the other night. He was toolin' around the bars, I suppose. He left with this blonde, hair down to her backside."

Now he's watching closely for my reaction. "That's nice," I say. "OK, well gotta get a move on. New refrigerators don't sell themselves."

"That's why you're goin' all the way to Shrenksville."

"Yeah. My fridge finally conked out."

Looking off his game, Mel starts to fiddle with the combs standing in the blue Barbasol liquid.

"Anyway, if Mr. Wu brings this Margot over here, please convey my very best wishes to them both."

He nods. He's holding a comb that looks pretty funky; Barbasol or no Barbasol.

CHAPTER 37

I'm surprised to see Esme still at the house. "We struck a deal," she says.

I don't ask. "I'm real glad you're stayin'," I say.

She pinches my cheek and we both grin. "Coffee, hon?"

"Sure, why not!"

We sit at the island sipping our coffees. Stevie-J could be anywhere by now. Most likely with the blonde and her long backside hair. I couldn't care less. Keeps him off my butt. Thoughts of sex with him have dried up. It's all shallow puddles then the sun comes up.

I'm happy and Esme seems happy. "You want a donut?" she says.

"OK."

She orders from the donut specialty shop *Donuts & Donuts*. For fun I say, "Are they from Donuts & Donuts?"

"Where else?"

I crack up laughing. "Hey, you want to hear a secret?"

She pushes the box of donuts toward me. "Tell!"

"Mr. Wu got married to Maybelle."

Esme gasps and makes the sign of the cross so fast

she knocks her coffee cup over. I grab the paper towels. "Mr. Stevie-J will go berserk. He'll kill Mr. Wu."

Again, I find this very interesting. Extreme, you might say. "Why should he care who she marries?"

But Esme just shakes her head looking more worked up. "Are you going to tell him this secret?" She's keeping her voice low.

If I don't, I'll have to drag my butt out of here every day conducting a fake search. Then again, if Esme is correct, it could be bloodshed. I've been put in a bad position. Stevie-J should take all blame for this. I think he's one of those guys who will stick his dick in any convenient hole. And, Margot, being an exotic dancer and escort and whatnot, I doubt she's very particular. Which gets me to scratching my neck. I think I've got a case of hives from nerves. I have screwed Stevie-J a number of times. If I hadn't, there would be no mansion or swimming pool or cars. I'd be sweating it out in the chicken house, getting around on my bicycle, wondering about my next meal.

"You know what, Esme, I think I'll keep it quiet a while longer."

CHAPTER 38

My good luck. Stevie-J stays out all night and doesn't appear in the morning. Esme gives me this news as I sit down at the center island. Grinning, I take my time with her perfect once-over-lightly fried eggs and crisp sausage links. No push to get on the road today. We drink coffee and chew the fat. Then I leave to change into my bikini.

The pool glistens. I could become a pale shade of this turquoise if I spend enough time in this water. It's an interesting theory I once heard about.

After a while, when I start to shrivel from so long in the pool, I take a lounge chair in the shade. Deliberately avoiding the sunny areas that Maybelle favored; particularly the lounge chair where she plunked her bare ass every day. If Stevie-J shows up, I'll have to tell him why I'm here and not on the road in search. I'm hoping the blonde keeps him very busy.

The noon whistle blows. Still no sign of him. I wander inside to have lunch with Esme.

"You just might be one of the sweetest people I ever met," I tell her. "And not because of your great cookin'."

For lunch today she made German potato salad from scratch, which she serves with sliced pepperoni-salami on pita sandwiches. "At this rate I'm going to put on the pounds," I say, stuffing her food in. Esme just laughs. So pleasant. I can't imagine being as pleasant with all she has to handle around here.

"The kitchen is the only nice room in the house," I say. "The rest looks leftover from Knights of the Roundtable."

"Stevie-J bought everything in here kit and kaboodle. Even the bed sheets and towels."

"Really!" To hear him tell it, he had the mansion custom built!

"Aside from his silly money making scheme, he's kind of lazy," Esme says. "He wanted a place in move-in-condition. This was the only house on the market that served his wishes."

He never struck me as lazy. But some men are when it comes to the domestic stuff. They expect the wife to do all the picking and choosing. He must be that type. If he had a baby, I can only say *good luck* to whoever the wife might be. Raelyn should consider herself blessed to be out of that situation.

"I was married a short time," I say.

"You, hon?"

"Yeah. His name is Clyde. He was a drug dealer. Still is, I guess. Since I knew beforehand I only have myself to blame."

"They're fly by night," Esme says. "But, you, hon, you're all class. You need a dependable man on the legit side." She scoops more potato salad onto both our plates. "I had myself a bad man as a young bride. He knifed somebody in a bar fight and they put him away."

"Jeez! Do you ever hear from him?"

"It happened out west. He's got no idea where I am. I even had my name changed. Can't be too safe these days."

"So Esmerelda isn't your birth name?"

She shakes her head but says no more. I respect that. A person tells what they tell and that's that.

"Esme, do you think it was a crocodile that he wrestled?"

She lets out a long howling hoot. "Hon, I think it was nothin'. Nothin' at all. Just some cheap camera trick."

CHAPTER 39

The largest flat screen is in the largest living room, along with the largest couch. This place has a few living rooms and I'm settled in the largest, stretched out watching *Friends* re-runs and thinking I might turn in soon. I can't remember having this much terrific shut-eye. Stretching my legs on the long, plushy blue couch I giggle, sort of wondering where Stevie-J might be. But not really wondering too hard. I hear a loud grinding engine; possibly the loudest imaginable, at least for this town. I've heard some super loud ones on TV in those monster truck shows. I have to turn the volume up on *Friends*. It's always when you reach the climax that something blows in smashing your chance to find out how things end.

The noise goes dead, then I hear chatter coming closer. A man and a woman. Almost like a movie when the opening music is still running. Then Stevie-J steps into the room, followed by the tallest woman I've ever seen. At least a half a head over him and he's no shrimp. Blonde hair running straight down to her ass. Real blonde. The most beautiful shade of blonde imaginable.

All sun streaked and thick. Not speaking, they both look at me.

"Hello," I say.

"Janelle, meet Leila."

She steps forward, putting out her hand. I reach up from the couch and we shake formally. She has to bend since I'm down here and she has all that height. "Hi," she says, then straightens up.

"How are things progressin'?" Stevie-J wants to know. Formal, too. Everyone so formal.

"They're progressing," I say.

"Good."

"Yeah."

"Is there anything you want to say specifically?" he asks.

"Do you have a few hours?"

"Not really." He looks at Leila putting his hand on her shoulder. I recognize the move. She pats his hand.

"I guess it can wait till morning. I'm pretty tired, myself." I force a yawn. "So you sleep well. Both of you."

If Stevie-J thinks this Leila will create a problem for me he is so wrong. I'm actually euphoric. Get married, I'm thinking. Raise a brood of brats.

They leave, and a few minutes later I turn off *Friends*. I should probably transfer to another bedroom. The one I'm currently using is on the same hallway as his room. I don't care to run into them and having to make small talk.

I lug my stuff up a long staircase to a bedroom on the third floor where the ceiling slopes. Because nobody sleeps up here, or maybe never has, no sheets are on the bed. I make do. Wrapping up in the huge fluffy comforter, drifting off.

There is someone in the room. I'm all of a sudden wide awake. A haunting up here under the eaves? But, no. He's found me. I groan telling him to go away.

"Janelle, can we talk a few minutes?"

I groan, again. He sits on the bed. I inch away though the bed is pretty damn large. "Can't it wait till morning."

"You *know something*, Janelle. I saw it in yer eyes."

"Turn on the damn light, Stevie-J. I can't tell you how much this annoys me. We had a plan then you wake me up out of a dead sleep. Maybe what you saw in my eyes is the pollen from your gardens." Over-planted, I might add. I mean every square inch of border or path—flowers and more flowers. It was like when I craved Oreos as a kid and Mama bought a box of them and I ate them all in one sitting. It was nauseating.

He gets up and flips on a switch flooding the room with yellow light. I put my arm against my eyes. "OK, you want it, Stevie-J, here goes. Your stupid sister has up and married Mr. Wu." As they say: you could hear a pin drop.

"Maybelle?"

"Is there another sister?"

"No."

"Then, yes."

"You tellin' me Maybelle married that wig lunatic?"

"Apparently so. Mel told me."

Stevie-J drops onto the bed, again. "This is a fucking disaster."

"Why? Maybe they're in love."

"Ain't you talked to Maybelle? Does she seem capable of love?"

He has a point. She seems like a store dummy. Head hair, and skin. Like before they dress it.

"Look, maybe they just hit it off. Two lonely people getting together. I don't know. Hey, aren't you concerned about leaving Leila all on her lonesome?"

"She'll be fine, I gave her good weed."

"Ah. Good weed." The savior of all that ails us. When I was ailing he didn't give me the good weed. I got the good dick. Leila gets the good weed. *Eventually it all comes out in the wash*, Mama used to say.

"Will you be fucking her after the good weed?"

"Janelle I liked ya much better before you came to live here."

"Hm." So is this my departure notice, my pink slip? I guess I'll find out soon enough. "Go back to Leila. She's very pretty, you can drown your worries in *her hair*."

"But I want *your hair*," he says.

I can smell his body. That's always the start for me. I'm very attached to certain odors.

"Janelle, just let me hold you a while."

He moves in fighting his way through the puffed layers of comforter. He's found my hair with his mouth, nuzzling into it, sucking on the ends for all he's worth. "I love your hair." It comes out garbled. "Your beautiful orange juice hair."

"Get off me!" With all my strength I push him away.

"What's the matter?" He's still buried in the comforter.

"I know what's on your mind. A fuck up here, a fuck down there. Forget it!!!"

His head pops out of the covers. "It's not like that with her."

"Oh you just keep her around for the intellectual chit chat."

"She knows Maybelle. She was tryin' to help. I have a whole SWAT team out there lookin'."

"But you brought this twat home."

"Well you don't want to fuck me anymore!"

"Stevie-J. You really need to ramp up on your lyin' skills 'cause they totally suck! You are so… I honestly have no words!"

He smiles then. Admission. He's a fucking liar. We both know it. Then what the heck— we do it. Long and hard and crazy.

CHAPTER 40

In the morning Stevie-J is still next to me. I poke him. "So what about Leila?"

"She'll be fine." He turns over, snoring lightly.

I get out of bed and wash up and head to the kitchen. Leila is fine. She found the kitchen and Esme is feeding her. "Good morning," I say.

Esme winks. "An omelet?"

Leila ignores me. I can see how she and Maybelle would be friends. They carry the same hostility. I get my coffee then sit two stools away from Leila at the island. "Esme, if you have any cheddar left I'd love it in the omelet."

"You got it, hon." The stainless steel fridge is enormous. The top with the double doors and a huge bottom drawer freezer. I s'pose there's cheddar enough in there for a year or longer.

When I was working at Mel's I read in the paper that the Mafia put a man's body in the bottom drawer of his own big freezer. No one could find him for months. Then it was like he never died once he thawed out.

Just as my perfect omelet is set down, Stevie-J comes barreling in. "You smell sweet," Esme tells him.

"I used this shower stuff in Janelle's bathroom." He grins and gets himself a coffee, taking an empty stool between me and Leila. "Good morning ladies."

"Hello to you," says Esme.

Leila and I just keep chewing. I think of two cows sharing a small plot of grass.

"What d'ya want for breakfast?" Esme asks him.

"A New York bagel?"

"No have got. How about a frozen croissant they bake off real fast."

Stevie-J gives her a thumbs up. "So I been doin' more thinkin'," he says. "You two will need to team up."

Leila's head jerks, and I can barely swallow what I chewed.

"It makes complete sense," he's saying, "since Leila knows Maybelle and Janelle knows Wu. So we team up and bring our own two-some. Double team their double team." He's laughing at how clever he is.

I gulp air a couple of times. My pool days are coming to an end.

Esme is struggling to open the cardboard box of croissants. She curses a few times getting nowhere. There's a lot of ice clinging to the box.

"Any dead people in the freezer?" I say.

They all stare at me.

"Give it here," he says. Cracks the box with one hand passing it back to her.

"So strong," says Esme. "That's how you wrestled that croc so good."

She's on his payroll plus she's not stupid.

"Yeah, well, the croc took a bit more strength." He turns toward Leila. "Whatchu thinkin' about?"

She shrugs and goes on shoveling the food in. At her height I figure she eats as much as Stevie-J yet manages to keep slim. It sort of annoys me.

"How do you figure we'll sneak up on Mr. Wu?" I say. "They know your Corvette, and Maybelle certainly knows the truck."

"Everyone knows my Corvette."

"Probably you should've bought a more neutral car."

"Why'd ya think I bought the blue truck? Blue. Not my silver one. No one in town has seen the blue yet."

Esme slides the plate of warmed croissants in front of Stevie-J. "Here's the sweet butter you especially like," she says.

"We have the blue truck and our team," he says. "We're a family."

I rest my chin in my hand.

"Are you sayin' you expect me and Leila to sneak up on Mr. Wu in the blue truck? Is that your plan?"

"Well, duh, Janelle. You get the gold star." He's slathering on the butter. "These croissants, for frozen, smell real fresh. Don't you think, Leila?"

"They're OK." She has become the new ice queen, replacing Maybelle. Her plans apparently didn't include sleuthing.

"Which of us will drive the blue truck?" I say.

"You my sweet. Leila only knows how to drive automatic."

"How convenient."

"Yep, it's for the two of you to find Maybelle, a snazzy blue truck with white leather interior. Now don't go drippin' any Taco sauce on my spanking new seats! Ya hear!"

The last thing I eat is fast food Mexican; a recipe for food poisoning. Everywhere you turn, these days, everywhere something's out to get you.

Half an hour later Leila gets her period and begs off. I'm waiting in the kitchen, can't prove she didn't get her period but I'm smelling suspicion coming off her aura. Which is an unfriendly yellow. Not blonde, like her hair, more a yellow with a green tint. Not a fresh minty green but more a sour pickle color.

Stevie-J wipes his hands together. "You'll have to do the first day on your own, Janelle. I can't risk my seats with Leila and her blood."

"You could put a Hefty bag with a towel over her seat," I say.

Leila refuses. "I'm bleeding heavy with terrible cramps."

How fucking convenient. I suppose I could say that I got my period, too. Slightly harder to pull off since I spent the night with Stevie-J.

Funny, but she didn't seem at all indisposed scarfing down Esme's food from Stevie-J's larder. He looks aggravated by this sudden switch in the plan. He's not the type to want a loser on his team. At least I've decided she's a loser. I could have pulled the same period stunt, or a dozen others. She came here for one purpose. And it wasn't to go on the road in search of Maybelle. "You have a greenish aura," I tell her.

Right away she gets defensive and tells me to fuck off.

"OK. I'll take the truck by myself, today. But only for today." That last part I deliver straight to Leila. "Best go back to bed and rest your blood flow." She glares at me. "Where's the truck, Stevie-J?"

Stevie-J demands a session with me before I head out. "What do you mean a session?"

"I have to give you the truck's basics."

Leila, meanwhile, is not to bed but goes outside to sunbathe. A Maybelle re-run. I'm standing watching her through the kitchen sliders. "Leila seems to have perked up."

He looks embarrassed.

"I think I can figure out what to say to Mr. Wu, should I somehow find him without a map."

"A map! The GPS Janelle! You tell WuWu that Stevie-J has a proposition for him."

"What proposition?"

"Just tell him that." He kisses my hair, rubbing his

nose in like a crazed rabbit. "I swear I get a burst of beta-carotene every time," he says.

Esme claps and asks when we're gonna announce the engagement.

"How about never," I say.

"Never say never," says Stevie-J.

CHAPTER 42

Mel is my first stop. *Start easy and escalate if need be*, Captain Cragan told Olivia on Law & Order. I'll pump Mel conversationally. Like I'm so damn bored with my new life I just couldn't resist coming by to chew the fat with him.

The door card is flipped to OPEN and the door is unlocked. But when I step inside Mel is nowhere to be seen. "Hey, Mel, you in here!"

I hear clopping from the basement stairs then Mr. Wu appears. I'm so shocked I jump back.

"Janelle," he says, "very good to see you."

Honestly?

"Mr. Wu! So good seeing you, too." Almost too good. This is too easy. "Is Mel around?"

All I need now is Maybelle to show and I ring up Stevie-J from the cell phone he gave me. Some old flip phone he had in a drawer but it works. He tested it before I got in the blue truck. He tested everything like I was going on army bivouac patrol.

"Is Mel around?" I say again.

"You didn't hear news?"

"What news?"

"Mel caught virus. In hospital."

I'm stunned. But why should I be? Mel being a stick in the mud anti-vaxxer. "How is he doing?"

"Not so good," says Mr. Wu.

There's some more clopping and Maybelle appears. This actually is a dream come true.

"Oh it's you," she says.

I stand there calculating my next move. "I guess it's me," I say finally.

It's obvious Mr. Wu is happy to see me, and that Maybelle is aware of it and she's less than happy that he's happy. That's all I can make of the situation at this point.

"So you both are keeping things ship shape until Mel comes back?" I don't say *if* Mel comes back. The big IF.

For late morning the shop is empty of customers. Mel *is* the shop. The screwballs come for Mel more than for what Mel provides. His haircuts are just so-so. Mr. Wu and Maybelle don't stand a chance on keeping the place going.

"We start new enterprise," says Mr. Wu, like he read my mind. "All wigs now. Selling like crazy."

So much for my theory. Looking around I don't see a Confederate drape anywhere.

"Who do you sell them to?" I ask.

"Wig magazines," he says. "Maybelle model the wigs. She look very beautiful in magazines pictures."

Her hair is now shorter-long, and kind of shagged, a streaky mix of black and auburn. "Is that one of your wigs?" I say, pointing.

"Yeah! Yeah! Big seller to older ladies. Make look young again."

Maybelle corrects him. "Make *them* look young again."

He's beaming at her.

I almost add: *Makes* them look young again. He called her Maybelle. Did she ditch the Margot alias?

"She help me with English." He looks deliriously happy. I don't recall this level of happiness from him when Mel was running the place.

I suppose I should congratulate them. "That's great," is all I can manage. "Well, very nice seeing you both."

Mr. Wu makes a polite little bow while Maybelle's eyes are darting. Heat lightning is her aura. Well, I did my job. I located them. Easy aces. Done. And goodbye Charlie.

The ride back in the blue truck is divine. I blast the A/C and the music. I'm thinking I should stop at Kenny Rogers for the plate of chicken and biscuits I never got that day.

CHAPTER 43

After my Kenny Rogers—less delicious than I remembered—probably 'cause I've been eating Esme's food which is so totally scrumptious—after finishing the Kenny's plate I decide to stop by the chicken house. Chicken and biscuits, the chicken house. It all seems to fit. I haven't been back in a while. Maybe Mel spread the word and the Klan burned the place down. Keeping mum about his possible involvement with the Klan, while I acted his devoted little employee.

Taking the dirt road I come out behind the place. In the high weedy grasses, the chicken house is standing same as ever; pitched a little; an old wobbly legged bird. I almost start crying. Not because it's standing or because it's not standing. Just because it exists. Because it's where I call home. No matter how much I trick my brain into believing I live in the mansion.

The door is still locked. That's a good sign. I step in. Not only is it hot as hell, now there's a strange funky smell I can't put my finger on. I walk slowly looking to see if any animals took their last breath here. I check the whole place and inside the two closets. The terrible smell is throughout. Worse in the bathroom, I think. But not a bathroom type sewage odor. Where the floor and wall meet behind the toilet I see tiny mushrooms growing in clumps. I bend and sniff. Sure enough—there's the disgusting smell. Mushrooms? How did they get in? Worse, how to get rid of them?

Under the sink vanity I find a bottle of laundry bleach pouring it over the mushrooms. They seem to sizzle— before shriveling up. As if they were alive the way I'm alive. That final sizzle—their last gasping breath? Mel comes into my mind. I picture him with a tube shoved down his throat. Biting my bottom lip I'm thinking *poor Mel*.

I close the toilet lid and sit down. I honestly think I'm starting to go insane. I should probably move far away. Forget this place, the town, people I've known my whole life. At least the funky smell is starting to fade, at least in the bathroom. Here I mostly smell bleach. I crane my head around the tank to see them. Disgustingly dead. Then I stand up, leaving the bottle of bleach on the floor.

CHAPTER 44

Back in the truck it occurs to me: *Janelle, you can just keep driving.* Like how Mama would transport her thoughts. Just clear the hell out of this state. The blue truck is a dream drive and the gas tank is full. What's to go back to, really? Eventually, Stevie-J will get bugged alerting the cops. They'll pick me up. Stevie-J, with his soft heart, will forgive my little joy ride.

'Cause deep down I'm starting to think he loves me truly. I wish I loved him back. It would simplify everything.

I head toward the interstate to take a last look at his billboard. Damned if I can make out what he's holding high above his head with clouds puffed behind him.

Then I lower the window and wave good-bye to Stevie-J's billboard. Time to make tracks. It occurs to me that I'm driving his flashy new truck with no more than my sack purse, two nearly tapped out credit cards, his VISA, and just the clothes on my back. I should phone him and give him the info on Maybelle and Mr. Wu. I'll do that. When I make my stop for the night.

It's a beautiful day for a long drive to somewhere.

When you can control your comfort level, everything else becomes *a beautiful day*. If I were driving up north in snow country, the heater pumping out toasty hot air, that would be a beautiful day. Money. Money makes the most beautiful day. These days it takes lots of money to feel even slightly comfortable.

I press a button and the moon roof opens. My hair blows wildly. Increasing the cold air conditioning, I'm thinking: I could do this the rest of my life. Just drive. This is what happens when you've been incarcerated. I been in that town forever. It wasn't a 4X6 cubicle with a toilet but at times it felt so tight I could hardly breathe. Same people, same stores, same schools, same playground, same Kenny Rogers, same movie theater. And, on and on and on…

A GPS is a terrific gadget. *A gift from God* is what the people in town might say. God this and God that. *God's Country*. Didn't he invent the whole planet? But you can't argue with the God people. You might as well bash your head against a wall. I'll keep driving till I clear out of the south. Who knows how far? I might even drop in on Sly. If I could find Maybelle and Mr. Wu that easy, how hard could Sly be? He's somewhere in NYC, I'm certain.

Burger King for lunch. It's not Esme's burger, but it's not too bad with ketchup and extra pickles. The plastic booths are mostly filled with moms and noisy kids. A good reason to hurry things along. I stop in the bathroom then head back to the blue truck. Cinderella only got a pumpkin carriage. This is a whole new century.

I start the truck and fish in my sack purse for the phone. Not feeling it, I empty everything onto Leila's seat. No Leila, now no phone. What the hell happened to the phone he gave me? Cursing up a storm I head for the highway. I drive until five-ish when I spot a motel that looks OK. Face it, you lived in the chicken house, I'm thinking. A barn and hay pile would work out, too, if it comes to that.

The guy at the desk says, "Standard or Superior room?"

"Oh, definitely Standard." I laugh. He just looks at me. He asks for a credit card and my stomach sinks. "Your card won't be charged until your last night is complete," he says.

Interesting. My travel experience being limited to Disneyworld. My short honeymoon with Clyde. He had a ball, loved every minute. Right then and there I knew it wasn't meant to be.

"My credit cards are in the glove box."

OK, the desk guy says and I can bring it later. Then he asks if I have luggage. My brain is churning. "In the hatch of the truck." Gotta start saying *my truck*. "I'll get that later, too."

I'll get it later than later.

He passes a stiff purple card across the counter. "Just push it in the slot. When the light turns green you can open the door."

"Yes, I know, that's standard." Which I didn't know. He nods; so I guess it is standard. "S.O.P."

"What?" he says.

"Standard operating procedure."

"Were you in the armed forces?" he says.

"Something like that."

Respect has crept into his eyes; I can see him turning this over in his mind.

"Not something I care to talk about," I tell him.

"If you need anything, just give a holler."

"Thanks. Bye for now."

Did he mean extra towels? Or was he pushing dope because I was in the armed forces? Even the armed forces probably have better accommodations than the chicken house. With its side of mushrooms.

I move the truck to a space right outside the room, on ground level. It's one of those white motels with aluminum siding. Not a good choice in this heat. Metal works like a cooker. I feel I need the truck close by. Anything can happen. Suppose the A/C in the room sucks? I can go out periodically and at least cool off in the truck.

The room is standard Standard. Everything bolted down. I take a breath. Well, I guess it's time to phone Stevie-J. Which will be less than fun since I no longer have a phone.

CHAPTER 45

Icall collect from the motel office phone. Esme answers. "Where you at, hon?"

"Oh, you know, here and there, been searching out Maybelle."

"Any news of her?"

Esme should only know all the news of her and then some. "I think Stevie-J should be the first, if you don't mind, Esme."

"Lordy, of course he should. I'll go get him. Stand by."

Esme would faint if she knew where I was standing by.

"He's comin', honey, he's takin' a soak. Should I hold supper for you?"

Ah, jeez. "No, that's OK, because I have to stop by my old place and get a few things."

"That's perfectly fine, hon." I can feel her smile in her words. She likes me, did from the first. "Here's our man!" she says.

"Janelle! I been waitin' all day. What's the story? Where are you? You OK?"

And something wicked starts brewing in me like dark smoke.

"Well, here's the thing. It was extra hard doing this for you, Stevie-J, on account of Leila punkin' out like she did. I had to figure out this move and that move all by myself with no one to bounce it off."

"Yeah, I'm real sorry about that."

"So, anyway, I suspect a lot of good time got wasted and I felt myself going in circles for a bit, trying to dope things out. Then I had a little lunch, and was starting to feel really bad thinking how can I go back to Stevie-J all empty handed."

"Are you sayin' ya got nothin'?"

"Keep your socks on. So I went on back over to Mel's. It's closed up, you know, he's got the virus bad."

"I told that old asshole to get the shots."

"I know you did, Stevie-J. I know you did your best. So I go to the shop—I don't know what made me go back there—it was almost a premonition. That other time the door was locked. And this time the door was unlocked. I walk in and the place is empty. No clients, no Mel to be seen. I shouted his name all the same. Then I hear this clopping up those wooden basement stairs, and who do you think is standing in front of me?"

"Mel."

"Don't be silly!"

"Janelle will ya get to the point!"

"Mr. Wu."

He groans. "What about him?"

"Mr. Wu was there. In the barbershop! Then more clopping and up comes Maybelle."

"Are you playin' with my head?"

"Of course not. When did I ever play with your head? It's downright insulting. You need to apologize."

"I'm sorry. Very sorry. Did you find out more?"

"More than they're married?"

The phone goes dead. In the motel office an old wall clock ticks near the check-in.

"Yeah, more," he says, like he's gritting his teeth.

"I didn't want to slam you all at once. I was going to tell it in segments."

"Just freakin' tell me!!!"

"Well apparently Mr. Wu and Maybelle have temporarily taken over the shop. To use as a wig place."

"They're makin' wigs at Mel's?"

"I don't know if they're making them in there, but apparently Maybelle is modelling them for wig magazines. She dropped the Margot, by the way. I assume Mr. Wu takes the photos."

"*Apparently* and you *assume*. Janelle, the law runs on tighter stuff than that."

"The law? Are you saying they're breaking the law?"

"Time will tell."

"Stevie-J, I have some things to do. My whole day was wast… taken up with this. So, anyway, I'm thinking of stayin' at the chicken house for tonight."

"You hate the chicken house, you said you hoped it burned to the ground."

"Well, yes, that is true. But I swung by earlier and there's a mean crop of mushrooms growing in there. From being closed up and all, in this weather. They stank. I figure I better clean them out before it becomes more than I can handle."

The phone goes dead quiet again.

"Hello! You still there?" I say.

"I'm here. I want you next to me. Tonight, Janelle."

What about Leila, she still bleeding? runs through my mind.

"Just give me this one night to clean things up and get rid of the mushrooms, OK?"

He agrees. But sounds really moody. I'm hoping he doesn't come by the chicken house and find it empty. I don't even know why that should really matter. When I don't show up tomorrow, all my cards will be out there on the table. Then, holy shit.

CHAPTER 46

Technically, since I'm a fugitive on the run, with no credit card to pay for the room other than Stevie-j's, I leave before sun up. I want to get as far north as possible each day. My desire to reach New York City is intense.

I also figure that each time I cross a state line, there is less chance of being picked up by the cops. When Stevie-J finally figures things out, and reports his truck missing, he'll have no idea what direction I'm going. At least this is how I understand the car hijacking stuff works. I used to listen when the old Judge came to Mel for his haircuts. The idea is to keep crossing state lines. Zig-zagging if you can.

I spot a Denny's and pull off the road, driving around back. Cheap food. A large cheap breakfast and a pile of cheap fast food for supper. Stay at cheap places. Leave before sun up. It should work out.

In Denny's a guy seats me in a huge tufted booth big enough for six people. "It's only me," I tell him. He's a cute guy with glasses. Probably goes to college at night. Looks to be the studious type.

"We're almost empty right now. You look like you have a need to spread out."

Jeez. I do have a need to spread out, to spread my wings. Exactly why I stole the truck. "That's so nice of you," I say. "Are you a college student at night?"

"You mean because I work in the daytime?"

"Well, yeah. And because you look smart."

"I'm farsighted," he says. "With astigmatism."

"Oh. Well you still look smart."

"I'm on probation."

My head jerks. "You mean like probation after serving time in jail?"

"Yes, Ma'am." He hands me the big menu. "I suggest you get the Denny's $3.99 all you can eat deal. And the sausage links cooked brown and crispy instead of the bacon."

"What's wrong with the bacon?"

"It was frozen a long time. I think it's past the expirey date."

"You mean the expiration date?"

"Yup that's the one."

"OK. Bring me what you said." I hand back the menu without ever opening it.

He walks off stiff in his posture. I wonder what he did to end up in jail? I suppose, technically, I could land in jail. If Stevie-J somehow found out my whereabouts, and the cops swarmed the truck. If Stevie-J decided to press charges. I have no one except him with enough money to bail me out. It's a pickle. I could end up on parole, too, working in a Denny's or similar.

The food comes out looking good. "Thank you." I can barely look up at him. Now that I know he's on parole, I'll be super careful about what I reveal. If he knew my situation, he could call the cops and cut a deal, I suppose. Maybe that would shorten his parole time.

"Would you like coffee or tea?" he says.

"I'll take coffee with Half & Half, please."

"Righto." Again that stiff walk. He may have had some trouble in jail, like what I've seen go on in certain movies. A shiver runs up my spine. I definitely would not handle jail well at all.

He returns with my coffee. "You haven't touched your breakfast," he says. "Is anything the matter?"

"No! Not a thing." I smile and start cutting the sausage. "It is very crisp," I say.

"I never touch it," he says. "But the expirey date on…"

"Yeah!" I say, cutting him off. I don't want to hear anything about sausages. Under any circumstances. I get busy eating and he walks off with that stiffness which kind of drives me crazy wondering. Anyway, I hope I didn't upset him. Not 'cause I care about him. 'Cause I'm worried about me.

CHAPTER 47

After Denny's, I decide to drive past all future Denny's along the route. I know it's totally paranoid. I don't want to take any risk. That prison guy must know other prison guys and they do communicate from a phone in jail to the outside world. He could pass along info on Stevie-J's truck. I'm starting to not trust a living breathing soul.

The drive is smooth with very little traffic and lots of strip malls with stores I never heard of. If I didn't have to make tracks north, I could stop and buy a change of clothes or two. But I can't take that risk. Parked in a lot, some cop could already have the plate number and description of the blue truck on his wanted list. Or missing truck list. Whatever cops call it.

What you're doing is a huge risk, Mama is saying.

"I don't need advice. But thank you all the same, Mama."

Forget that I've driven past two states—she's still coming at me! I believe it was Mama encouraged me to sign the monthly lease on the chicken house. She didn't have to live there!

Two states past now; which probably makes me an official fugitive. Exciting in an odd way. Probably the Denny's guy who went to jail thought his gig was exciting too. Until he got the body cavity search.

Janelle there's still time to turn around, Mama says.

As dusk rolls in, along with some fog, I stop for the night at a place called Link Log Cabins. It should be up in Vermont where they drill the trees for maple syrup, not some backwoods place down south. All those logs look strange in that piled up way.

When I ask for a standard room the desk girl tells me she only has small cabins available.

"Of logs?" I say.

"It is our theme."

True. "How many rooms in the cabin?"

"One. It's a one room small cabin. With an outdoor shower."

"Does it have an indoor toilet?"

"It does now. And a little round sink."

She gives me a price and we barter a bit. "I just can't afford it," I say, playing on her sympathies. I'm sure she has money troubles, too, otherwise why'd she be working the night shift here.

"I wish I could, but they'd fire me." She seems truly sorry. "Look," she says, "there's a cot in the back room." She points to a room behind her, which is part way open. All I can see is darkness beyond the door. "You can sleep there. It's put there for me to take little cat naps but I never do. I'm always afraid there could be a stick up while I'm sleeping."

That makes me gulp. "Is this a place of many stick ups?"

"We get our fair share."

"Then I guess I better say no thank you." I smile and she smiles back sweetly.

"That's a beautiful truck ya got there. Looks brand new."

Jeez! This girl notices everything. What if a cop strolls in, some local, to chew the fat with her, flirt a bit, and she mentions me sleeping in the back and how the cool blue truck belongs to me. Then the cop happens to recall that six state alarm Stevie-J put out, I'm sure. By now it has to be at least six states he's trackin' me in. Was the girl hinting that I can easily afford a small cabin because the truck is fancy schmancy? Definitely not the place to spend the night.

I tell her I think I'll drive through the night, after all. We say *goodbye* like long lost friends. She must be lonely, I'm thinking. "Are you married?" I ask.

"Not anymore."

"You?"

"Never could get up the courage." A lie. But who wants to continue this topic of conversation? It was real dumb of me to engage her in chat. I feel the need to move on, and quickly at that.

I drive about five miles from Link Log Cabins and pull off the road into a little cove of thick trees. I should be OK here, hidden in their low hanging leafy branches. I lock down the truck and push the seat all the way back. Not bad. All that's missing is a light blanket. The night has brought a slight coolness on. I hug myself to stay warm.

In the morning I'm feeling too skeevy for words, though I didn't sleep badly. Considering. I'll order an Egg McMuffin when I spot a MacDonald's. After chowing down I'll ask for the bathroom key. All the fast food places seem to lockdown the bathrooms. Back home that wasn't the case. This is a big country. Lots of trouble brewing. The Link Log Cabin girl mentioned a fair amount of shoot outs. Anything can happen at any time in this country. It's like the wild west. I really need a shower. My new blue truck also needs a washing. *My truck.* How I've come to think of it.

CHAPTER 48

When I finally do get to New York City, I'll go to the library and use one of their computers to look up Sly in the White Pages. I just know that's where he's landed. Sly wanted that city like it was a fix. He always called it The Big Apple which seemed kind of corny at the time. Now I get it. He needed something big and juicy and shiny as his way out. Out of the tightness of that box called home. I guess he talked about it so much his desire rubbed off on me. And I don't know much about the place other than the giant tree at Christmastime with the skating rink, and the countdown on New Years Eve in Times Square. I'd also like to see the Empire State Building. My life, added up, is a big pile of zeros. My checkbook balance is proof enough.

A MacDonald's sign looms ahead. The south is so freakin' predictable till it's not.

I park behind the building near a clump of shade trees. Today I'm feeling philosophical. Things are either this or that but never the best parts of either: Say Leila hadn't gotten her fake period. If she'd been with me, the journey would be over. I would not be on the road as a possible fugitive. But back at Stevie-J's mansion in the same rut; a luxury rut but a rut all the same.

Scarfing down my Egg McMuffin I become aware of a pair of eyes locked on me. A lady with two boy toddlers smiles when I glance her way.

"I was just noticin' your hair," she says. "Ain't seen hair that color in natural since I don't know how long. Plus God gave you the thick curls. He must love you a lot to bestow such gifts."

Ah, yes, god loves me. Straight to the chicken house and possibly on to jail.

"Why, thank you Ma'am." She should know how bad my scalp is itching in need of a vigorous shampoo scrub. "I happen to be on my way to the beauty parlor, long over due for this curly red mop to get some attention. And maybe a few inches chopped off."

Her hand moves quickly to her throat. I didn't say my head was being chopped off, just a few inches of hair.

"Hon, if I had that hair, on this head, I would keep every inch. Even if it grew to the floor."

"You have very pretty hair," I tell her. Which isn't exactly true. It's too short and dyed a frosted brassy blonde. It makes her look forties into fifties. While she's probably only late 20's or early 30's. Who would do that to themselves?

"Thank you," the woman says. "Howie, he's my husband, well he just loves my hair all pouf and blonde. My real color is light brown." She puts a finger to her lips. "Don't tell anyone."

"You don't have to worry about me." Who the hell would I tell? She must think I live around here.

"I'm Arlene," she says. "From over in Junction."

The first name to come into my head is Chillin' Millie. Which is, of course, too weird even for a lie. "My name is Milly," I say. "With a y."

"Such a cute name!"

I shove the final bit of Egg McMuffin in. This conversation is getting a tad personal. I read that New Yorkers are much more aloof. They don't even look at you on the subway, just going about their business. Not like the south. In the south everyone's busy pokin' their nose in your affairs. I'm not exactly thrilled she spent so much time on my hair. Suppose Stevie-J convinced the law to tack up an *America's Most Wanted* flyer in the post office? He has lots of pictures of me. My *America's Most Wanted* could travel through the entire southern part of the country. Those cops just love Stevie-J. What he says to them is religion. If this Arlene from Junction saw it in her post office, she would naturally alert them.

I pack up the fresh orange from my tray in the napkins. "Saving for later," I tell the woman who seems to regard me as her new *BFF*.

"You got a little eggie on the corner of your mouth." She's touching her's at the corner.

I brush it away with the back of my hand. But this Arlene isn't done, she's just warming up. "With that figure you could be a model," she goes on.

Like Maybelle? I feel like asking Arlene if she'd like a red wig the color of my hair. Then send her on down to Mr. Wu and Maybelle. It's just a few states.

I shove the wrapped orange in my sack purse, wave goodbye and scoot out of the booth. I can hear her telling the little boys: "There goes a sweet girl like the one I'll never have."

Why can't she have a baby girl? Did her husband die or leave her or something? I can understand a man leaving that sort of woman. But, no; she said Howie loves her hair.

I move at a sprint to the truck, toss in my sack purse and jump in the seat. That woman has totally unglued me. Her eyes on me every second. Ignoring her two little boys. Maybe she's not a lonely woman but some kind of investigator. I put the truck in reverse too fast, squealing the tires. Like today her childcare worker doesn't show up, so she's forced to bring the kids. She seemed more interested in me than in them. What kind of mother??? They ate their little food and mumbled to each other. Nobody cried. Dr. Phil said kids remember every last thing. These kids might remember their mom saying she would never have a little girl child. And they might remember the sadness in her voice. Damaging to kids, according to Dr. Phil. I'm trying not to be paranoid but Arlene could also be damaging to me.

Two miles down I take the highway ramp as the GPS instructs. Some of the guys who came into Mel's believe that a type of GPS lives in the virus vaccine. That if you get the shots the government could track you everywhere. Who would want to follow *those losers* around?

CHAPTER 49

For the first time since leaving the mansion I consider turning back. I'm driving on the big mother-fucking four lane. In a technically stolen truck. Or Stevie-J may have reported me as carjacked. Me and his truck. He can be very calm about most things then gets outlandish notions in his head. He may even be on to my New York City plan. I do have a tendency to ramble. If the cops ask *Where do you think Janelle is headin'?* he just might say to New York City.

I'm feeling so raggedy-ass filthy. There's no way of telling right from wrong, truth from fantasy, when you live this way. I'm not exactly enjoying my days and nights. One thing is clear. I need more clothes and a good hot scrub. Do I miss my life at the mansion? Yeah. But that wasn't *for keeps*. It was a time-out. With certain provisions. Like sex when Stevie-J wanted it. Which kind of made me a kept woman. No better than Maybelle. Or even Leila who he's probably screwing regularly now.

A semi passes blasting his horn and I see this guy who looks like an axe murderer, all scruffy and ugly and he's giving me the finger. Whew! Probably another jail bird like the Denny's kid. Those guys get out and head straight for the tractor trailer jobs. Good money, anonymous lifestyle. Again, I think about turning around. But then I'm right back where I started. Stevie-J and his extreme sex drive. Says he was born that way. His Daddy did a lot of steppin' out on his Mama. He said it was on account of a testosterone overload and that I shouldn't get down on his daddy. That overload may have passed through the genes.

CHAPTER 50

Rain mid-morning adds to my already damp mood. GPS, who I've named Grant Peter Stud, has instructed me to leave the highway. Good. I'm sick of seeing semis wheeling toward me doing ninety-plus and spraying my windshield to blindness. I'm driving blind, mostly. Not all that exciting. I want to live to at least 35. I want so many things I can't begin to name them.

Now when Grant Peter gives me a route, I acknowledge his knowledge. I feel it's only fair. "Thank you, Grant Peter," I say, as I drive into a small town. The rain has stopped and it's all kinda pretty with baskets of hanging geraniums off the light posts. And quite a few shops and cafés. The sign said: WELCOME TO MAGNOLIA. I bet there's maybe 50 towns in this part of the country named Magnolia.

"Stud," I say, "where can we find a cozy little motel for tonight on the cheap?" Somehow it doesn't get through to him. It's funny with men—they jump on certain things and ignore your most crucial needs. I try again. "A motel in Magnolia. On Fishing Street," I add, since that's where I happen to be. But, silence. Maybe Stevie-J didn't program it entirely.

I drive into a gravel lot next to a park with big looping trees. Kids are climbing and hanging like monkeys. In the tall bamboo surrounding Bingo's Karaoke patio, that night, I had thought a monkey would make a bold touch. That night feels like ages ago. I mark that night in my mind as the start of my journey.

Walking the quaint streets people say *hello*. It's a custom down south but really the hello doesn't mean a goddamn thing. In an old time drugstore called Barnett's, I find a box of body wipes fragrance free. These will be good to freshen up after a night in the truck. I'm anticipating many nights in the truck. I can sponge down with them and feel fresh. My hair is a whole other operation. When it turns really funky, I will have to knot it up top my head.

While paying for my wipes at the counter, I ask the young, pale freckled guy if he might know a nice place for me to bunk for the night. He shakes his head up and down a bit longer than normal. Not that I would know normal if it bit me. Plus I'm starting to feel ghosts on my back. The law.

When the young guy says, "I've got a garage band," I just nod. "No practice tonight. For twenty bucks you can sleep on my air mattress."

"Does that include a blanket and pillow?"

He's thinking. "OK."

"Where do you live, nearby I hope."

"Next street over." He writes the address on a blank prescription pad.

"Isn't that a doctor's pad?" I say.

Again, he takes some time before answering. "My pop was a doctor."

"Did he retire?"

"Not quite."

"Well why do you have his prescription pads here?"

"Comes in handy," he says.

I notice his one eye drifts from time to time, leaving too much white near the nose.

What kind of freak is this that I'm planning on paying twenty bucks to sleep in his garage? Jesus! I scratch my neck.

"Lice?" he says.

"Of course not!"

"Sorry. I thought you might want the de-louse potion."

It's like a pie in my face. I guess I look pretty skanky to the world of the showered. Gathering my composure, I say, "Grant Peter likes me earthy. Dig?"

"Your boyfriend?"

"My bodyguard."

People have lined up behind me. They're tired of waiting. "C'mon, sister, get a move on," some guy shouts. Others are voicing their frustration, too. Loudly. Crudely, even.

"Pay them no mind," he says. "Do we have a deal?"

"Can I fit my truck in the garage, too?"

"You never said nothin' about truck storage. That means I gotta clear out all the band stuff to fit your truck. That's another 30 bucks."

"Do you need advance notice?"

"OK, lady!" A man from the line is next to me, freaking out in my face. "Whatever your STD, Junior here ain't in no position to offer medical advice. Get off the damn line!"

Junior? "Your name is Junior?"

I move out of the line. You never know. This is a carry state. People start clapping. "I may be over later," I tell him, leaving the store without my bag of wipes but not realizing until at least half an hour has gone by.

CHAPTER 51

A cute café on a street that climbs called Hill Street is where I park my butt. This is the first time I've felt a little human and part of the human race since I began this new life style. Everyone here at the café is so nice. The boy who brings my ice water, the waitress who sets up the standing menu black board next to my table. I order fried fish and fries. It comes in a cute basket with a blue checkered cloth napkin under the food. There's a little side salad of crisp lettuce and cherry tomatoes. Everything so cute. I want to stay here till morning and have a cute breakfast. But of course that can't be. As I dunk the fries in ketchup, I'm still debating about Junior's garage. I forgot to ask the specifics: Like is it attached to a house or a separate garage on its own? Something about a separate garage is a big turn off. There could be mice, rats, roaches, flesh-eating spiders, chiggers and the likes. I'm not in any mood for vermin. Vermin would put me totally over the edge.

After the lovely lunch, I order dessert. A slice of key lime pie made in heaven. Big and so creamy delicious it makes me feel teary for Esme and the huge kitchen.

Those comfy stools along the wide island. And, of course the turquoise pool. I'm always carrying that pool on my back. It filters through my dreams. I read that water means emotions. That pool like an old lover—and you can't quite cut the cord.

There's still time to kill before Junior's house. I sit a while longer, my truck (my truck!) parked on a quiet secluded back street. This is what happens when you start to believe the lie. You start to seriously own it. I feel ownership over the truck which is my sole companion. I once knew a guy who loved his old crummy VW Bug so much he named it Red Baron. I heard he cried real tears when the car junked out forever.

I check the address Junior gave me, asking the waitress if it's nearby. She points in a direction over my shoulder. "Only a few streets," she says. "Y'all can get there in under five minutes."

"Oh, well that's good," I say. Realizing I've just disclosed my whereabouts to a perfect stranger. At least my possible whereabouts. A stranger who could possibly be questioned by the law. Instinctively I touch my hair. Its carrot color and thick curly tangle and long length—you may as well wave a big red flag. *Here I am, come and arrest me.* I have to do something drastic with my hair. If this waitress sees my *Most Wanted* flyer, I am so totally fucked.

Junior's garage is attached to a standard one level ranch style house. In fact the garage door is wide open. A typical suburban neighborhood for these parts, with their scraggly lawns and a few scrawny trees planted here and there. For a moment I think of the gardens at Stevie-J's and the emerald lawn that could be in a magazine. Here the driveway leading up to the garage is empty of cars.

I decide the safest thing is to back up the driveway. It makes the truck look more like it belongs here. Not some transient truck. When it's your truck and your driveway, you do what you want. Most people park head in. Though, maybe this backing in is a bad idea. Just the position of parking backward, out of the ordinary, might alert someone on a search for me; and the truck. I think Stevie-J would be more inclined to put out a search for the truck. When you come right down to it.

At the curb I'm debating. Then Junior is out there waving me up. I have no choice but to drive up normally.

"Do you own this house?" I say, slamming the heavy door shut.

"Now that is what ya call a truck. Jeezers!"

"Yeah. So do you live alone?"

"With my Ma and Pa."

I stand there still as a rock. What made me think otherwise? Junior is still wet behind the ears. "How old are you?"

"Almost twenty-one. Coming up on legal drinking age, so don't you worry about that."

"I'm not worried. Just curious." The place seems so quiet and deserted. "Are your parents away?"

"Ma's gettin' supper and Pa's still at work. He works over in Kluge in the button factory."

"A button factory?" Who gives buttons a thought? I guess they have to make them somewhere. "Do they make a lot of them?"

"Millions."

Millions of buttons. Must be shipped all over the world. I suppose some person would have to be in charge when the buttons reached their ports of call. "Junior did you clear me with your mom and dad?"

"Yep. Ma said fine. Pa will go along."

A man who will *go along.* I'm not entirely familiar with that breed. Stevie-J sometimes went along if he sniffed sex at the end of the trail. Men are like dogs, in a way. You have the happy ones that never are displeased with you, and vice versa. But most dogs are always searching for something to put in their mouth.

I peer into the garage. It's still filled with band stuff. A large drum set takes up a lot of space. The truck is a goner. It will have to stay on the driveway. "Where will you fit me?" I say.

Junior walks into the garage. I follow. "Well, I was thinkin'. How 'bout this spot here by the bike racks. Ma says you can have the futon."

Now I'm totally unsure. "When the door closes, there's no air in here, right?"

"More or less." He scratches his head. He's a red-head, like me, but a light shade, with a short red beard just on his chin area. I don't have the beard. Yet. I'm getting so grubby I s'pose a beard isn't entirely out of line. My whole body is starting to feel like it's shifting into an abnormal zone. All this stress and strain, the crap meals, the uncertainty—can all lead to hormonal imbalances. I could start to develop male traits. Like a beard.

"So you stayin'?"

"I'm thinking."

"Nights here are cool. You won't sweat to death."

"Oh. That's good to know." I'm weighing my options. "So which is your instrument?"

"All of them."

"That's a joke, right?"

"Nope. I play them all."

"But you have a band so you choose one for that night to play when you play out. Right?"

"I am the band," says Junior.

It's almost too much for me to absorb. And I've seen some real crazy stuff.

"So you're playin' guitar then the bass line comes in and you drop your acoustic and grab your bass? What about the empty noise?" I just said *empty noise*. How weird is that? I'm also feeling kind of light-headed.

"In between I play harp. To keep the progression."

"You mean a mouth harp?"

Junior nods. "So what's it gonna be? You stayin or leavin'?"

I feel my eyelashes batting all on their own. "I guess... I guess I'm stayin'." I stare around the odd garage. In its way no odder than the chicken house. "I

"Could you leave a few inches open at the bottom of the door?"

"You'll have rodents slip in."

"Close the door all the way."

I'm wishing I could figure out how to camouflage the truck.

"Ma says you're to take supper with us."

"Really?" What if they're a cult? You can't be too sure. It is America.

"She's a good cook. Pa bought her a big air fryer for her birthday and she's in there right now fryin' up those chicken parts."

More fry. Just my luck. "Thank you, Junior, and please thank your mother."

"You can call her Ma. Everyone does."

Ma.

CHAPTER 53

She seems to be a genuinely sweet lady. Pa comes home from doing his button thing and he is very polite, too. I don't sense *cult* coming off them. Or any kind of pressure toward me. If they were part of a cult, they'd be pushing me to stay in one of the spare bedrooms. Those cults indulge in misbehavior right off the bat. These people seem happy enough to have me at their supper table and sleep in the filth of their garage.

But Junior was right. Ma's food is amazing. Even the veggies and potatoes come out of that cooker with no grease. It almost makes me want to learn to cook.

I notice Junior is fairly quiet during supper which is served in the fake-wood-paneled kitchen. Just one window makes the tight room kinda dreary. A café curtain with a valance, yellow flowers on white cotton, and a little flounce at the bottom being the only decorative touch. Not even one of those *Home Sweet Home* plates hangs on the wall. I can't help but compare this to the kitchen in the mansion. You could put at least eight of these kitchens into that one. And still have space leftover to dance. Why am I comparing? Seems low, and petty. These perfect strangers have opened up their food and their hearts to me. And their garage! I can count on one hand how many people…

For dessert Ma serves orange sherbet swirled with vanilla ice cream in these old fashioned glasses with long glass stems and a curly q rim. It's very refreshing. Pa never mentions the buttons once, which is also a relief. I tell them my name is Eunice.

The garage situation, when actually confronted at bed time, is nothing to write home about. Not that I'll be writing home, or anywhere, any time soon. Junior sweeps my area with a push broom before putting the futon down. He also gives me a thick velour throw blanket with a basketball player rim dunking the ball. The pillow is foam with a clean pillow case.

"Anything else?" he says.

"What if I have to use the bathroom?"

"You just lift the door by that silver handle on the bottom and it slides right up. Then you're outside."

A piss or shit in the bushes. That's what he's trying to tell me. "I guess your family locks the house at night."

"Yeah."

"That's OK," I tell him, all perky sounding.

"Look, Eunice. I was wonderin'. You think I could ride along to New York City with you? I'd be no trouble. Plus I've saved almost ten thousand from my job."

He wants a ride to New York City. This is a conundrum. I feel a little shocked. Don't quite know how to answer. Though the ten thousand sounds like a share situation to me. "Do you have a credit card?" I say.

That has been my biggest worry. Stevie-J tracking me down by the card when I need to gas up.

"Three Visas," says Junior. He looks proud. "All paid up in full."

Three Visas! Could make an enormous difference. "Let me sleep on it," I tell him.

He nods, saying, "Do ya want the door closed before I leave for the night?"

"Yeah. If you don't mind."

"Not in the least," he says. "Here's a flashlight. In case you need to go out."

I flick it on when Junior leaves. It makes weak light. The big door rolls shut with a bang.

CHAPTER 54

Next thing I know there's pounding on the garage door. From the futon I yell "Who's there?"

"Me, Junior." For a moment I thought maybe Pa had flipped his game and was coming for me.

"Oh, Junior!" A relief. And the garage, actually, wasn't bad. The futon is puffy and I slept OK. He wants to know if it's all right to open the door.

"Yes, it's OK," I yell back.

The door begins to roll up and the darkness is replaced by full glaring sunlight. I think in a next lifetime I will choose a place like Norway to live. Without a swimming pool, I'm simply not compatible with the sun. I shield my eyes, saying, "Good morning."

"Hello, Eunice. How'd you sleep?"

"It was good, Junior, thank you."

"Ma wants to know if you want a shower and breakfast?"

Uh oh. This is where the cult-ing might begin. Kindness and affection. In real life nobody does this for a stranger. They make you beg for your essentials. "Is that OK with your Pa?"

"He's gone off to work. Ma said the bathroom is free."

My instincts are telling me nothing. And now that I need Mama, she's skipped out. "Gee, that's real nice of your Ma. Tell her I said so. OK?"

Junior nods. "Call her Mrs. Ma if that makes you more comfortable."

He leaves the garage. I feel surprisingly awake. Mrs. Ma! Huh! The pool at Stevie-J's crosses my mind again. *Fuck* I say—no point clinging to what you don't have. Right now I have a truck (still parked there!) plus an offer of food and cleanliness from Mrs. Ma.

She left a big fluffy lavender bath towel and fresh bar of Dove soap on the vanity. Inside the shower there's shampoo and even conditioner on a pink plastic thing hanging from the shower rod. The bathroom is a pink and lavender scheme.

I get in and scrub top to bottom then scrub top to bottom all over again. While I'm waiting for the conditioner to work on my hair, I brush my teeth in the shower. I don't want to cause extra work for Mrs. Ma by messing up the nice clean vanity and sink. I carried my toothbrush and toothpaste into the shower in a baggie. It's my new tramp way of life. Gotta keep up with the teeth no matter what else is neglected.

Then, stepping out, I put my original clothes back on and style my wet hair in a long braid.

In the kitchen Junior is sitting at the table. Mrs. Ma working the stove. The perfect little family scene.

"Good morning, Eunice," they both say, though not exactly at the same precise time. "Did you sleep well?"

"Yes, I did, thank you so much for your generosity and hospitality, Mrs. Ma. And, you too, Junior," I add. Even though the house doesn't belong to him—he did hatch the plan.

My own home life was never Hallmark chirpy. Mama always busy hatching some scheme to make money. Once she hooked up with a super-vitamin pyramid scheme, until those vitamins were found to be loaded with caffeine. *Energy* was their advertising logo. No wonder Mama was always flying around the rooms crashing into things. I wonder if she's still flying around in ghost land.

"Dear, would you like some eggs and hash browns?"

"Mrs. Ma that would be so yummy."

"If you like coffee, just help yourself to the Mister Coffee Machine."

"Thank you again."

At Stevie-J's nobody ever said thank you. It wasn't expected. Esme got paid for her work. I did tell her when I loved something she'd cooked. Mrs. Ma seems put on earth to make people happy. That's a new one on me. "Sit at the table with Junior and these will be done in a jiffy," she says.

I take the chair across from him. He smiles at me but doesn't speak. I eat the food put in front of me and it is very good. Hearty breakfast food. Mrs. Ma slides a plate of toast next to my main plate. "Butter or jam?" she says.

"Butter, please."

"I knew you were a butter girl. Didn't you know that, too, Junior?"

He nods.

I'm a butter girl? Oh, well. "This toast is so nice and crunchy," I say.

"That's how Junior likes it," says Mrs. Ma. "Personally, I like a softer paler toast, myself."

Chewing, I gaze around the kitchen. It's brighter

with the morning sun coming through the space in the café curtain. But could I spend my life in such a kitchen? No possible way.

After breakfast and a second cup of coffee, I get up and hug Mrs. Ma. "I have to get going now," I say. "You are a wonderful lady."

She looks a little teary, as if I'm her daughter about to leave the nest. "Will you do me a favor?" she says.

Uh-oh. A cult after all? "Um… sure."

"Will you take Junior with you?"

Now I'm totally stunned. And more than slightly freaked. Her expression is serious. There's no smile or joking coming off Mrs. Ma.

I look toward Junior. He says, "I always wanted to get to New York City."

"You have?"

"I want to take my band."

His *band*? He said he was the entire band. I'm confused. I say, " I'm confused." Besides, how could I fit an entire band in the truck?

"Junior does it all," says Mrs. Ma. "All by himself. At the same time." She smiles lovingly at her son. "He's a genius."

He told me all this already. Did they put something in my coffee?

"There's room enough in the hatch for the equipment," he says. "I checked it out this morning."

"You got inside the truck! I was positive I locked it."

"It's locked. I looked through the windows. I can get by with just the snare, two guitars, bass, and keyboard." He pats his pocket. "And of course my harp."

He's mapped out the whole deal. How can I say no after they bed and breakfasted me? Of course it wasn't exactly luxurious accommodations. But he doesn't strike me as a serial killer. Of course, that's what they said about Ted Bundy. Just a regular guy. Junior looks like me. Pale skin red hair. Someone eager to make tracks for reasons of his own.

"OK. You can ride along."

Mrs. Ma takes me in a bear hug. "You'll never regret having Junior by your side."

I hope not, I'm thinking; giving her a shaky smile.

CHAPTER 55

I open the hatch so Junior can load his stuff. My legs are a little wobbly. This was meant to be me and only me.

In no time he's got everything fit in snug. Almost like *this* was meant to be. He tosses some extra drumsticks and two tambourines on the floor back there.

"You play tambourine?"

"Whatever it takes," Junior says.

I sit on the futon waiting while he gets his clothes together, coming out shortly with a duffel bag that he fits in the back hatch, too. It's all so easy. Kind of unreal. No fussing, or moving one thing to fit another in. Like there was a plan on paper and he's just following the steps.

Mrs. Ma has come outside carrying a picnic hamper. "Just some baked goods and apples for when you two might get hungry and need a little snack time," she says.

Junior puts it on the back seat next to his duffel. "I guess we're set to go."

"Do you need to use the bathroom?" asks Mrs. Ma.

"I guess it couldn't hurt," I say. "Just be a minute."

When I come back out she's disappeared and Junior is sitting in the passenger seat.

"Where's your Ma?"

"She doesn't cotton to teary goodbyes."

Smart. Teary goodbyes don't do anyone a bit of good.

"This truck is swank," he says.

"I know." I start it up backing down their driveway.

"How's the gas mileage?"

"Not that great."

"Good thing I brought my money."

I stop the car at the corner. "Junior, are you absolutely sure you brought your money?"

"Eunice, I'm sure. Do you want to see my bank book?"

"OK. I think that will settle it and there won't be any tension over the issue."

He reaches into his windbreaker and pulls out a check register. A little over ten grand. Like he said. "That should do us well," I say, turning the corner heading toward town then onto the interstate.

Junior puts on the radio. He actually chooses a station I would have picked. "Good one," I say.

We both settle back in the seats. It's going to be

a long trip to New York City. Having Junior here so far seems OK. A male travelling with a female adds a safety factor. I did worry some redneck might see me driving alone and try forcing me off the road. It's not that uncommon. Junior has a long neck, a bit too long for his frame, which makes him look really tall sitting down. A small scrunchy guy wouldn't pull the same weight as a taller man, when it comes to personal safety on the road. Suddenly I'm glad to have his company.

I crank up the A/C a notch. With Junior onboard I won't have to pump my own gas, either.

CHAPTER 56

We're getting along well, so far. Been on the road six hours with one stop for lunch. He mostly stays quiet. Sooner or later, I suppose, a conversation will strike up.

It happens when we exit the interstate and catch some heavy town traffic in Slomenville. "How do you think these names got started?" I say. "Like Slomenville? It's ugly. I wonder what the original folks were like?"

"Probably it started with bugs called Slomen that eventually died out," he says without hesitation.

Does he truly believe that? "Is there a way to find out?"

"Well, I s'pose if you searched the web you could find some Slomen photos of the original bugs."

Interesting. Slomen. It makes sense. Slomen, and this was their village. "I picture them living in mud mounds," I say.

He doesn't respond, bouncing in the seat to some tune I don't recognize.

"So, Junior, what's your real name? Your given name?"

"Wilbur. After my Pa. But then it got confusing so they started calling me Wizzy. It's a nickname for Wilbur."

"Wizzy is a terrible name."

"I started to go crazy," he says, "I felt like the world was spinning around me all wizzy. Ya know? You ever feel like that, Eunice? Like you're walking through the spinning barrel at the funhouse?"

"No! I couldn't take it."

"They were talkin' about putting me in the asylum out in Cartersville. Then Ma got the idea that the Wizzy name was causing all that trouble. So they called me Junior and I could walk a straight line again. Right behind my Pa." His face turns proud at the mention of his dad.

"That's such a sad story."

"I'm sorry, I didn't mean to make you sad."

"Not sad sad, but somewhat sad. You wanna know something? My real name is Janelle."

"Eunice is prettier," he says. "Hey look out!" Something furry and low to the ground nearly got squished by the truck tires. Which happen to be huge.

"Thank god you saw it Junior!" I'm shaking at

the thought of... I don't like the idea of hitting some innocent creature forced off its native land to make roads for big tires.

"Ya want me to drive a while?" When I don't answer he says, "Pull over by that church."

I pass it. Sooner or later down here, there's bound to be another church. "So many churches," I say. "Do you go to church, Junior?"

Then sure enough. I pull into a church parking lot.

He's getting out of his side and we switch.

Junior is not stupid; not by any stretch. He has a quiet command of things, as I'm beginning to notice. Stevie-J has a command but totally different. His is about what he can conquer. All sex driven. While Junior may still be a virgin or possibly gay. He has no interest in me whatsoever. Not in that way. It's a relief. We're like a sister and brother combo. Janelle and Junior. It's comforting. I didn't know I needed comfort till I drove away from what I thought was my comfort zone.

He's a good driver, very steady. "Nothing wizzy about your driving," I say, making a joke. He laughs then says he needs to make a bathroom stop.

"May as well get lunch," he says, driving up the ramp off the Interstate.

"If you could measure all these Interstates, combined, what do you think it would come out to?" I say.

"The width of the Indian Ocean."

"Seriously?"

"No."

I laugh then, whacking him lightly on the arm. "Oh, you are a wizzy at times."

"Only when I'm tipsy," he says.

"I can't picture you tipsy."

"You'll see. One of these days I'll get tipsy and drive this truck into a wall."

"Junior, that's a joke, right? You are makin' a joke?"

He looks surprised that I would even consider it other than a joke. "Eunice, you don't trust me." He does look truly hurt. I don't think he's faking. I've seen fakers most of my life and can usually spot them cold.

"Junior, please accept my apology. But, you know, you hardly ever make a joke so when you do it takes me by total surprise."

He's shaking his head. "Yep, yep. I can see that."

After supper in one of those all-you-can-eat spaghetti joints, with the red checkered table cloths and fake flowers in a bud vase, we sit over coffee like an old married couple who no longer has sex. Not that we ever did or ever will.

"So what is your dream when we get to New York City, Junior?"

"My band."

"You mean your one man band or an enlarged version?"

"Me, myself, and I."

I start to giggle. Feeling light and less encumbered. I am not a good one man band. I realize this now that Junior has signed on with me. I'm glad I made the decision to take him along. And he does have that spare ten thousand which for me ain't exactly pocket change. Not that I plan on dipping into his funds. But it's a nice cushion till we get to New York City and find employment.

"I've never seen New York City before. I would imagine they've got a gazillion people with bands." I say this 'cause I don't want him to be disappointed if his one man band doesn't take off there.

Junior slurps the last of his coffee. "Have faith," he says.

Then, out of nowhere (where she always is but less frequently lately) Mama pops up, says *He's a good un.*

I tap one foot on the floor. "What's that tune you're tappin' out?" he says.

"I forget the name."

"How does it go?"

"You want me to hum a little?" Of course I know the tune, I know it cold. *Colder than a witch's tit* Stevie-J would answer.

I hum the first line of *Suzanne.*

"That's Suzanne by Cohen," Junior says. He's all lit up. "You hum nice, Eunice."

I shrug. "If you say so. Maybe you should start to call me Janelle." I stand up. The bill is paid, time we split for the road. "Let's hit the road while there's still some daylight left."

"Bet you can sing it real pretty." He follows behind me out to the truck. The sky is less heat violent. That could change at any time and we'd be back to the cooker.

"So what about it," he says.

"Another time."

"I can play harp to accompany you." He pulls the voice harp out of his shirt pocket.

I start the truck, backing out. "Why do they call it a harp when it's a harmonica?"

Junior's already tucked it into his mouth and the soulful sounds of *Suzanne* fill the truck. "You do play really good, Junior."

"So you gonna sing that song for me?"

There's a small bit of traffic. "All right. But if the traffic builds up, I stop singing. We can't crash this truck. It would be the end of my life. Even if I don't die."

We start our little duo act. When I finish the song he takes the harmonica out of his mouth and stares at me. "I had no idea," he says. "You've got the voice."

"Oh, well. That's nice of you to say, but I'm ordinary."

"Eunice there's nothin' ordinary about your voice. As Ma would say *You got the gift and God delivered it purposefully*."

If those words had come from Stevie-J they'd be the beginning of… I push him out of my mind. First 'cause I'm still afraid the highway police will pull up next to the truck at any moment. Second 'cause he still makes me feel hot and bothered.

That's a curse you're carryin' Mama says.

"Don't need you reminding me!" I yell.

"What?" says Junior.

"That wasn't meant for you."

He's on a happy high. It was the music. In our few days together I've not seen him look so happy. He's bright like those oranges from China that Suzanne brings her lover along with tea. Frankly I don't see that combination of foods. If I eat an orange, I don't have a cup of tea. Even afterward. Still it is a great song.

"Junior we need to rustle up a place for the night. Any ideas?"

"Ask the GPS," he says.

"You can do that?"

"Sure."

You'd have thought Stevie-J would have laid a little more instruction on me, before giving me the truck to stake out Maybelle and Mr. Wu. That could have taken me weeks, even months. They might not ever have been found. Did he expect me to live out of the damn truck? Leather seats or no leather seats. It's quite outrageous.

Then I picture Maybelle and Mr. Wu and what the hell they've been up to?

Junior finds us a Nifty Inn with discounts. "Only 3.7 miles up the road," he says.

"Good. 'Cause all that singin' wore me out."

CHAPTER 58

I stand surveying the small twin-bedded room. "If this is quality I'll eat my Mama's Birkenstocks."

"It's not that bad." It comes out garbled. Junior bought some gum from a machine in the lobby and is chewing about four pieces.

"Can you play harmonica and chew gum at the same time?"

He falls back laughing across one of the beds. I was a little hesitant at first. But then a 50% discount on twin rooms. What could happen? It's not like I'm a virgin or anything. It's not like I'm anything.

"Junior, you should be careful, you could choke on that much gum lyin' down. And I ain't good with the Heimlich Maneuver."

"It doesn't work on gum." He's laughing harder, all garbled from that wad stuck in his mouth. Finally he sits up and smacks the gum onto the wooden headboard. *"Does your chewing gum lose it's flavor..."*

"What would your Ma say if she saw you put gum on the furniture?"

"But she doesn't see." He pulls out his harmonica

playing the rest of that crazy old time tune about putting your gum on the bedpost overnight. "Sing along, Eunice."

Oh, what the hell. He's got us both so goofy now. I sing the words to his harmonica playing. He does it three times. When it's over we're both collapsed in hysterical laughter.

"We should get some wings," he says.

"I cannot eat another bite. That spaghetti is buildin' a cement wall in my gut."

"See you did it again."

"Huh?"

"Talked low south."

He's back on the harmonica playing that same dumb tune, then stops dead in the middle and pulls off a pillowcase and shoves it over my head.

I grapple with getting it off, then snap it at him making wild animal hisses. "You jerk!" I can't stop laughing.

"Your face is really red. See, Eunice, you are the blushin' bride!" And he blows out that damned tune again.

"Go across the road and get your greasy chicken

wings. I'm watching some tube. I need a break from you. Go on! Scat!"

He leaves the room wearing a big grin. I go in the bathroom to change into the one thin terry cloth robe the motel has hung on the door hook. Two beds, one robe—a faded shade of peach from many washings. It even has a wear mark on the pocket. It will have to be my pj's for tonight till we can get to a store. I can't sleep in my underwear now that Junior's slinging along.

I settle into the bed farthest from the door and put on *Friends*. There's some big commotion going on between two of them—I think that's the story. I'm not a regular viewer so I tend to confuse the plots. Pretty dumb plot, if you ask me. Getting pregnant after the divorce. After the divorce you grab what you can and head for the hills. A bit like what I'm doing. But the show is funny and making me laugh and the bed isn't too sunk in. This kind of motel never changes a mattress until someone falls asleep with a cigarette burning it up.

I'm lying here finally in a real bed, enjoying myself, relaxing, when there's pounding on the door.

"Open up Janelle I know you're in there!"

Stevie-J! How the hell… we parked behind the motel. He bangs a few more times. Clutching the robe at my neck I get out of bed. Behind the closed door I say, "Yes?"

"You know who this is. Don't play games with me, Janelle, I'm not in the mood."

I move the swing latch and he pushes the door open so fast I have to jump back. "You almost flattened me!"

Stevie-J steps into the room.

"What do you want?"

"My truck, for starters."

"You can have your truck. It's parked 'round back."

"I'm aware, Janelle."

He's here. Big and tall. Furious. I never saw him quite this way. He's certainly nothing like Junior who is thin and gentle.

"Will you be taking the truck now?" I say. I'm thinking *Take the truck and get out of here.*

"Actually, no." He smirks. "In the morning you are going to drive it home, Janelle, because I have this other car to drive home. The one that got me here. But I'll be up your ass, all the way. No sneaking off in traffic for you."

Already I'm no longer afraid of him. "Fine," I say. "When in the morning?"

Junior comes in holding a white food bag. "When in the morning what?" he says.

"Who are you?" says Stevie-J.

"That's Junior," I say quickly. "He hopped a ride with me. For safety sake."

Stevie-J gives him a low lidded stare. Not friendly, not unfriendly. More like curiosity. "For whose safety?" he says.

"Why mine, of course," I say.

"Good thing you took off," says Stevie-J. "'Cause everything turned fuckin' insane."

"I thought you were mad I took off."

He grabs me in a big bear hug, practically weeping. "Thank you Lord," he says.

Junior holds out the bag. "Wings?"

CHAPTER 59

According to Stevie-J the chicken house disappeared into a deep sink hole in the ground. Only a slight portion of the top is visible. The Town Council decided it was a goner. *No point trying to yank it back up*, the Mayor had declared.

"What a hullaballoo," says Stevie-J. "The whole town thought you were in there and went down in the hole with it."

"I coulda been." But for the antics of Mr. Wu and Maybelle. "Did anybody send down a search team looking for me?"

Stevie-J coughs. "Janelle, nobody would have survived that."

"But nobody tried to find me."

"Deep down I felt you out there."

"In God's ether?"

"No, out in the world."

Anyway—apparently they started placing flowers and pictures of me singing Karaoke and some other mementos. Stevie-J said someone took the standing microphone from the Karaoke bar and placed it near the hole. But not too close for fear of setting off another sinkhole. Someone even laid down the old toe-nail clippers from Mel's.

Meanwhile Junior and Stevie-J have camped out on the other bed sharing the chicken.

"Relatively speaking," says Stevie-J, "it was almost as impressive as when Princess Diana died in the car crash in that tunnel. And all what followed."

"I wasn't born then but I saw it on a TV movie," I say.

"I saw that, too," Junior says. "It was a tragic thing."

And all this time I've been thinking I'm a fugitive.

Junior had spread a towel over the bedspread to catch any grease. Unlike Stevie-J who has Esme to pick up after him, Junior is very tidy. "Good wings," he says.

Licking his fingers Stevie-J grunts his approval.

I sit on the other bed watching them. This trip has made me into a watchful person. At Mel's I did my best to not watch all those cranky geezers.

I get under the covers. The days are still hot but the nights go down fast to chilly. Now they're talking band stuff. Stevie-J asks to see Junior's equipment. They finish off the wings and go outside. I turn off one lamp. All of a sudden I'm just dying for sleep. I'm halfway there, when they come back to the room.

"So, Junior here tells me that you're on yer way to New York City."

It comes through me like an echo chamber. "That was the plan."

Junior says, "Eunice and I." He sounds disheartened.

"Eunice?" Stevie-J starts totally cracking up. "She's a Eunice like I'm a eunuch."

Unfortunately I'm disturbed to the point of being fully awake now. "Eunice happens to be my alias," I say. "But forget it. I'm no longer on the lam." It was exciting and it was awful.

He comes to my bed and lies down close since he has no choice, the bed being narrow. "Maybelle and Wu are having a baby," he says.

"That's not exactly news."

"I think it's a boy. Little Wu."

"I hope they'll be very happy," I say.

"'Course they will. Livin' off me."

"You have them at the mansion? What about Leila?"

"Leila jumped ship about the same time you did, Janelle."

"I suppose you upset Esme so much that she split, too."

"Who is Esme?" says Junior. He crushes the wings bag and tosses it in the waste basket. "Who are these people?"

"Who are they? Why, all these people, one way or another, they're Stevie-J's groupies. Except for Maybelle who is his sister." Of course it's all debatable.

Stevie-J corrects me: "Half-sister."

"Whut – evah."

"So we gotta make a plan here," says Stevie-J. He's managed to squirm under the covers and I feel his hand roaming. I poke him hard with my elbow, which makes no difference, then squirming away I fall to the floor.

"Ouch that hurt." I stay down a few minutes to consider things. "I'm getting dressed and getting on the road. You comin' Junior?"

"Whoa! Hold it there a minute, you two. Both cars belong to me. Ya can't just sashay outta here in one of my vehicles. I can only take so much, Janelle. Next time I will put out a state to state. And when they find you, well good luck."

"Isn't that how you found me?"

"Hell no. The state couldn't get yolk out of an eggshell. My publicist gave me his personal P.I. You want results, Shelby is your man."

Results. I'm down here in this crummy bathrobe.

"Janelle, you really look like hell. You look like a Eunice. Beautiful women need care and attention." He gets out of bed and pulls me to my feet in a bear hug.

Over his shoulder I can see Junior. He's a blank.

"Here's the plan," says Stevie-J. "We give Junior the truck since he's got his equipment stashed in there. He'd never make New York City on the bus with all that stuff."

"He still has his drum set back home in the garage."

Junior, surprised, appears to be having an out of body experience. His vacant eyes go bright. I almost expect him to float up hanging around the ceiling. "You kidding me?" Junior says.

"No, man. I never kid about important stuff."

"How will I get the truck back to you?"

"After you become famous you'll contact me and I'll send somebody to pick it up. You'll have some hot truck of yer own by then."

"How do you know he'll become famous?" I say. "And what about me? I was the one you said would become famous. You forget pretty fast, Stevie-J. I'm still going to New York City."

"You'll both become famous. In your own time and your own way."

"How do you know?"

Stevie-J does this movement of the hands. "I do. And that's that."

"Well." I wiggle out of his grip. "So where *you* gonna sleep tonight Stevie-J?"

"With you, baby doll."

"I don't think so! You're a big guy and this is a very small bed. Not what you're used to. Not at all."

He stands there rubbing his chin. "I s'pose I can always sleep on the floor... or..."

"Or what?"

"Well, on the trail to come get you, Janelle, I gave a lift to a little Indian gal also workin' her way north."

"Workin' how? On her back?"

"Janelle that's crude. Till you've met a person the Lord says thou shalt not judge."

So that's his *or*. Already has her stashed. "Where is she, next room over?" I want to say *your little harlot* but that would start up another religious tirade.

"Stevie-J, go sleep with your Indian woman."

"She's got a name. Pagan."

"Ain't that fitting! Go sleep with her."

Junior springs to his feet. "No way!" Gently pushing Stevie-J toward *his* bed.

"Man, I can't take your bed."

"'Course you can, Stevie-J. You're my main man. Besides, I'm used to sleepin' on the floor, I sleep in the garage with my instruments all the time."

"It's true," I say. "He sleeps in his garage to be near his instruments. On a futon."

"Usually a sleeping bag," Junior says.

Stevie-J shoots him that big famous smile. "Youse a good man, Junior. We gotta do somethin' about changin' yer name. You need somethin' stronger for a musician, like maybe… Digger." I notice he's peering at Junior's lazy-eye.

I can't picture Junior being a Digger. But Stevie-J, so awash in benevolence that he almost can't see straight—almost drowning in his kindness and goodwill toward this struggling young musician, is beaming. And that Pagan he's been forking—chalking that up to some benevolent gesture, too, I suppose.

He lights some weed, offers it to Junior.

"No thanks man, but thanks all the same."

"Plus we could put you in dark shades," he's telling Junior.

He takes a long pull. "I'm gonna give you a crash course in fame. Why?" Before Junior can open his mouth Stevie-J says: "Because I like you. The both a you." He tickles under my chin.

I ignore this.

He leans back against the headboard. "See, first you gotta ask yerself a simple question. And that question is: what do people take most of their photos of? Not countin' family members."

"Food," I say.

"Junior?"

"I'll guess food, too."

Stevie-J is laughing so hard his Adam's Apple is doing a jig... "You two are rubes when it comes to fame. Food? Who would take a second to look up at a billboard over the Interstate if I was holding up a corn on the cob?"

We're both silent.

"Nobody! That's who!" He grins. "Go on, take another guess."

I groan. "Stevie-J, do we have to?"

"If you want to learn the basics of fame it would be a good idea." He's into his squinty-eyed shifty look. "And don't say birds or flowers. Nobody gives a shit about them. Not for fame, anyways."

I shrug. I'm tired. Junior doesn't speak, either.

"The reason I held that croc over my head is because nobody, nobody, has the guts to even touch a croc. Never mind holding it over their head for the world to see."

I stifle a yawn.

"The croc brought my fame. And, all the money."

"What if you picked a lion instead?" says Junior.

"You gotta pick what people in your area are most scared of. There, it's alligators. Crocs being one step closer to hell. Have you seen any lions window shopping around these parts?"

"I guess not," I say.

"You guess not is correct!"

"I've never seen a single croc or heard about one down there, either." My mind has wandered to the sinkhole where the chicken house came to rest.

"Are you challenging me, Janelle?"

"No, but I haven't."

"See, that's yer problem. You can't think outside the box. Suppose I were to tell ya that the croc was brought in specifically for my photo shoot."

"They brought in a live croc?"

There's a pause. Then Stevie-J lowers his voice. "Did I say it was live? Did anywhere on that billboard state the croc was alive when I held him up?"

I pull the covers over my head.

"You two wannabees get the picture?"

I've heard enough. More than enough. "I'm going to sleep." Turning off the night table lamp again.

"Here, at least take the pillow," Stevie-J is telling Junior. I peek out and see him bashing Junior with it. "That won't make you into an addict." He takes a long hit on the pot then laughs at his dumb joke.

"Thanks, man," says Junior. Or should I say Digger. Then some more chat over the croc and how it was sort of alive. Apparently drugged into unconsciousness to be able to take the picture. I don't ask what happened after that.

Finally they kill all the lights.

I lie there in bed, the washed-thin bathrobe scratchy against my back, my eyes stretched open in the dark as if by rubber bands. Staying perfectly still until I hear Stevie-J snoring. Once he's down, he is *so* down.

Soundlessly I slip out of bed, carefully feeling around the night table, lifting my sack purse off. Stepping slowly to avoid Junior down on the floor. I have to bend over to make him out in the dark room. I whisper close to where I think is his face. "You comin'?"

Quiet as a mouse he rises from the floor and we two tiptoe out of the room.

***Hair of a Fallen Angel* is a sharp-eyed,** funny tall tale about an age old longing to escape small town life to become someone bigger. We follow adventures of the marvelous Janelle who is pretty amazing right where she is. I couldn't wait to see what would happen next in this rollicking, smart novel.

Alice Elliott Dark, author of *Fellowship Point*

Meet Janelle, a girl with flame-red hair and singing chops who rides an old Schwinn, lives in a ramshackle house with a mosquito problem and takes up with the crocodile brawler, Stevie-J and his magenta Corvette. It's a high stakes twosome for a girl who cuts toenails in a barber shop and sees herself as invisible as corn waiting to be shucked from the husk. Tepper's alluringly visceral prose engages the reader's senses—the heat and honeysuckle, the stickiness of waffles topped with ice cream. Ready for a date with destiny shinier than a karaoke bar, Tepper's Janelle, the girl who never thought big, is a joyous creature whose light illuminates the novel's darker corners.

Stephanie Dickinson,
author of *Blue Swan Black Swan: The Trakl Diaries*

Susan Isla Tepper has the gift of empathy and insight into disparate lives. And she further has the gift of being able to illuminate those lives with sharp, emphatic prose. In this new book she employs unflinching bravery and a clear-eyed honesty that makes this working-class, first-person voice compelling. It's literary seduction. I'd follow her struggling musician protagonist anywhere.

Corey Mesler, author of *Memphis Movie* and *The World is Neither Stacked For Nor Against You: Selected Short Stories*

This new work by Susan Isla Tepper blends humor with pure soul in a truly eloquent manner. Her novel is a prime example of true dedication to the craft. She manages to show the side of life where one can be down on their luck, yet still reflecting hope with a biting sarcastic edge. No mistaking Tepper is an artist of the highest level.

John Patrick Robbins, Editor In Chief, *The Rye Whiskey Review*

***Hair of a Fallen Angel* is a humorous,** delicious romp, start to finish. Packed with whacky, well-drawn characters, ingenious plot twists, and unexpected pathos, this brilliant, quirky novel both moved and delighted me. I didn't want it to end. Fingers crossed Tepper is writing a sequel. I can't wait!

Alexis Rhone Fancher, author of *Brazen*, *Triggered*, and *The Dead Kid Poems*